SNATCH

Scott Hildreth

Published by
Eralde Publishing

Cover Design Copyright © Creative Book Concepts
Text Copyright © Scott Hildreth
Formatting by Creative Book Concepts

ISBN 13: 978-0692665541

DEDICATION

Children.

Pay close attention to them.

They grow up to be adults.

The really heinous people we see on the news?

The serial killers, murderers, rapists, and complete ass-hats of society?

They were children once.

And no one paid attention.

PROLOGUE

An elderly man peered down at the glass of the display case. "Brandon, when are you expecting you'll receive the new Tag Heuer Professional series?"

Dressed in business casual attire, the man stood from his position of leaning over the top of the display case, looked at the jeweler, and smiled as he waited for a response.

The jeweler met his gaze. "Well, they should have been here by now. Let's say next week for sure. You won't be disappointed, that new bezel they're using is quite a compliment."

The elderly man grinned and turned to face the door. "Alright. Well, I'll stop in next week then."

The door buzzer sounded, indicating the arrival of a new customer. As the elderly man walked toward the door to leave, a young man in his early twenties walked in the jewelry store. Dressed in slacks, a freshly-pressed dress shirt, and wool blazer, the young man appeared to be a young business professional.

The young man walked toward the display case marked with the *Rolex* insignia. As he placed his hands on his thighs and bent over to gaze through the display case, he smiled.

The young man pointed through the glass at the watch on display located in the corner of the case. "The stainless *Datejust*. I'd like to see it again, please."

The jeweler walked toward the corner of the case. "You've had your eye on that watch for some time. You a man who recognizes quality, that's for certain."

The jeweler reached into the case, removed the watch, and held it loosely in his left hand. With his right hand, he reached into his apron, removed a cloth, and polished the watch before handing it to the young man.

The young man looked at the watch admiringly. In the last two years, he had frequented the jewelry store, admiring watches and saving money. Finally, he had reached a financial point that he was able to purchase this watch, and was ready to do so.

"Try it on."

The young man admired the watch. "I've tried it on several times, Sir."

"I know you have, several times. Try it on again. A man with a quality timepiece on his wrist is a man that exudes success. Let's see it on that wrist of yours, son."

The jeweler leaned over the counter, pushed his glasses up his nose, and smiled.

The young man carefully slipped the watch over his wrist and snapped the clasp. As he rotated his wrist to admire the face of the watch, his mouth formed a slow smile.

"I'll take it." The young man beamed as he spoke.

"Excellent choice. You've been eyeing it for years. Beginning today, your life will change. You'll feel like a success, and you'll become a success. Mark my words, son. Twenty years from now, you'll be one of Wichita's most successful business men. What are you studying?" the jeweler asked.

"Psychology. I'm going for a doctorate," the young man responded.

The jeweler looked up from the register. "That will be sixty-one hundred and sixty-nine. Forget the change."

The young man swallowed the lump in his throat. "*Six* thousand?"

Embarrassed, the young man lowered his head. He had wanted the watch for years, and the previous price, to the best of his knowledge, was five thousand dollars, not six.

"It's the stainless steel, not the two-tone," he said.

"Oh, you haven't been in for a while. Rolex had an increase. They do it about every ten years. They just increased it by almost a thousand dollars. It's awful, I know. Let me grab the box and warranty paperwork," the jeweler responded.

The young man removed the watch from his wrist and held it at arm's length.

"You no longer want it?" the jeweler asked in disbelief.

The young man reached inside his wool blazer and placed his cash in the inner pocket. "I want it. I can no longer afford it. Maybe in six or eight more months,"

"Put that watch back on your wrist, son. Today you're starting a successful life. I don't have a layaway plan or any form of loaning programs, but for you? Hell, you've been coming in here for years. Put that watch on, give me whatever you have, and when you get the rest, stop in and give it to me. Deal?"

The young man stared at the jeweler, uncertain of what to do.

"Well?" The jeweler chuckled. "You better hurry up before I change my mind."

The young man slid the watch over his hand and onto his wrist. After he snapped the clasp in place, he reached into his jacket pocket and removed the money he had saved.

The young man handed the jeweler the money. "There's fifty-two hundred."

"Let's call the difference a thousand, sound good?" the jeweler asked.

The young man looked down at the face of the watch. After a moment of admiration, he shifted his gaze to the jeweler and smiled. "Yes, Sir."

The jeweler extended his right hand. "I'll keep the box and paperwork until you pay it off. You're set to go. Enjoy that watch."

"I don't need to sign anything? Any form of guarantee to pay?" the young man asked.

"I trust you. This will be the beginning of a long lasting relationship."

As the young man shook the hand of the jeweler, he felt successful. This, in a sense, was his first business transaction. His first of what he hoped would be a lifetime of many.

The young man turned to face the exit. "Thank you,"

The jeweler nodded and smiled.

The young man walked to the door and pushed it open, hesitating before he stepped outside.

"Hey son, have you got the time?"

Filled with pride, the young man looked down at his wrist. "Ten minutes after ten."

As he walked toward his car, for the first time in his life, the young man began to believe that this was the beginning.

And that he would become what his father insisted he would never be.

A success.

CHAPTER ONE

TAKE TIME TO SMELL THE FLOWERS.

ONE. Walking up the sidewalk toward the front door, Ryan's nostrils flared; attempting to detect a hint of the honeysuckle he often enjoyed as a child. Frustrated at the lack of scent, he turned the doorknob, pushed against the unlocked door, and entered the home.

As he walked into the kitchen, he greeted his mother. His relationship with his mother had changed since he had become an adult, and he now cherished her thoughts and expressed opinions. Still dressed in her nightgown, she prepared her first cup of morning coffee.

Somewhat preoccupied and counting the minutes until he was going to leave, methodically he walked to the refrigerator and pulled open the door. As he mentally prepared an inventory of the contents of the refrigerator, the frustration began to build inside of him.

She peered over the top of her coffee cup. "Your slacks look nice, Ryan. Are they new?"

Ryan sorted through the objects in the refrigerator. "Yes, and thank you, mother."

Frustration began to turn to anger. It had been eight days since he last abducted a woman, and a newly chosen victim would be needed for the game he intended to play. Preoccupied with the thought of the woman he had been stalking; he realized what he was searching for in the refrigerator did not exist.

He stood in front of the refrigerator holding the flavored cream cheese in his hand. "At what point in time, mother, did you make a decision to exclude plain cream cheese from the list of necessities?"

"It tastes good, try it," his mother responded as she walked into the breakfast nook.

Ryan placed the container back into the refrigerator. "I care not for flavored cheese, mother. We've discussed this. *Plain.* I prefer the plain. Pineapple is a wonderful fruit, and I am quite certain it belongs in a kitchen. Where it does *not* belong, however, is in my cream cheese."

The anger began to build.

"The honeysuckle looks fabulous. I was disappointed at the lack of scent as I came up the walk. Maybe it was the breeze this morning," Ryan mumbled.

She shrugged. "It goes through stages. Sometimes it does, sometimes it doesn't."

They sat quietly at the table, facing the flower garden. As he nibbled at his bagel, he looked through the window at the flowers. Spring has always been his favorite time of year. The honeysuckle in the yard had been there since he was a young boy. The scent remained something that was calming to him. He had not lived in the home for thirteen years, and at times he missed it more than others. Spring was one of those times.

"I love the flowers, mother." The words escaped his mouth before he realized that he intended to speak.

She held her coffee cup as if her hands were cold, her palms pressed firm against the porcelain. "You always did."

Ryan recalled the scent of the flowers as a child, and the comfort they provided him as he grew up.

"How's business?"

"Investing? It's risky, mother. It's risky. I have been fortunate. I must go, I have to migrate to the office, my day awaits me." He pushed his chair from the table. "Resolve the issue with the cheese, mother."

Simple things aggravated him.

She did her best to jokingly furrow her brow, a light smirk covering her face as she did. She tilted her head to the left and turned to face him. "It's good, you should try it."

He kissed her cheek. "I love you. I'll see you in a few days."

"I'll tell your father you stopped by."

He placed the coffee cup in the sink. "The cheese, mother."

"You should try it," she repeated.

Ryan became frustrated at the thought of the flavored cream cheese, and her efforts to force him to try it. New things, to him, were difficult to accept. Stepping onto the walkway provided a hint of the honeysuckle and a moment's satisfaction from the scent filling his nostrils. As he opened the door of his car, he looked around the neighborhood.

Childhood memories returned. Simple times provided simple pleasures and learned lessons. Pleasures now came with a greater degree of difficulty. With each day that passed, his pleasures became more difficult to obtain. The lessons he learned as a child, however, formed him into the man he was today.

The lessons.

The coffee Ryan's mother prepared had not provided the same level of satisfaction as the coffee from a local shop. As he pulled into the parking lot of his favorite coffee house, he wavered between going inside and driving through the express drive-thru. The fact that he didn't see Ami's car in the employee portion of the parking lot caused him to second guess going inside. The length of the drive-thru line made his decision easy. Today, of all days, Ryan had a schedule he must adhere to.

Carefully, Ryan parked his car on the edge of the stall at the end of the lot. As he stepped out of the car and onto the parking lot, he turned and looked through the glass structure, and into the establishment. He smiled as he noticed Ami behind the counter.

Ami, a twenty-two year old employee of the coffee shop, waited behind the counter as Ryan approached. As she recognized him, she smiled a smile of satisfaction. She found Ryan to be intriguing – and although he was unaware, she was very attracted to him. The previous night, as she prepared her new hair color, she had thought of Ryan. As she had prepared to color her hair, she sat and wondered when she may see him next. Although she was in a relationship, she believed it to be close to ending, as she and her boyfriend had had begun to fight more and more.

Ami smiled as he approached the counter. "Good morning, Ryan. You look fabulous. The usual?"

"Good morning. Yes, and thank you." Ryan returned a smile as he reached into his pocket.

"No, this one is on me. We took forever to get you out of here yesterday." Ami waved her hands over the cash register as she spoke.

"No, I insist," Ryan murmured as he reached into his pocket.

She chuckled. "Your money's no good here."

Somewhat embarrassed and frustrated, Ryan reached into his wallet to retrieve a tip. It was important to him that he provided the store *something*. He did not accept hand-outs, reserving them for those that needed them. He reached into his wallet and removed a ten dollar bill.

Ami looked at the floor and shifted her weight on her feet, trying not to stare.

Her hair was a range of colors, her tips in contrast with the remaining portion. The two contrasting colors weren't uncommon – and were always perfectly mismatched – her primary color always brunette. She was tall and thin, yet curvaceous. She had exceptionally large breasts for a thin girl, and was an avid runner. Her translucent blue eyes looked down at the floor as Ryan broke her attention.

He forced a ten-dollar bill into the overly full tip jar. "Thank you, Ami. Your hair – it's the one thing that may be more beautiful than your eyes. You got it done last night, didn't you?"

Ami smiled as she turned her head to the side, feeling a little embarrassed. As she began to turn her head to face him, she stopped, hoping that her new tattoo was exposed enough that he could notice it. She had recently had a star tattooed behind her left ear, and although Ryan was extremely perceptive, he had yet to notice.

"Is that a new tattoo?" Ryan asked.

She smiled and moved her hair. "Shush. We're supposed to keep them covered. Yes, I got it last weekend. My brother did it. He's kind of a tattoo artist. It's a star. To me, it's the North Star. I hope it provides me direction."

She handed him the cup of coffee. "And yes, I did my hair last night. Do you like it?"

Pleased at the amount of conversation and the above average time in preparing his drink, Ryan continued to admire Ami. "I do like it. It's amazing you did it yourself. Multi-faceted you are; and I like the tattoo. Your brother? Interesting. I'm going to pry myself away from you and get to my office, Ami. Thank you for the coffee, your generosity doesn't go unnoticed."

"Well, my brother did tattoo's until the 9-11 thing happened. He joined the military as soon as that happened, and now he's a cop. He does tattoos at home sometimes, for family and friends. And, thank you, Sir," Ami responded.

Sir. The recognition could be good or bad. Ami was sweet, regardless of her intended placement of the word *Sir.* Ryan turned toward the door and thought of the word and the meaning it may have to *her*. As he carefully stepped toward the door, he wondered of his next victim's schedule as he took a sip from the cup.

Perfect.

Methodically, he walked to his car, carefully taking another drink from the cup of coffee. A few inches of coffee removed from the full cup would ensure none would be spilled in his car during his morning trip.

To Ryan, not much was more satisfying than a flavorful cup of coffee. The caffeine soothed his mind, and allowed him to think clearly. He placed the coffee cup in the cup holder and started the car. As she began to back out of the parking stall, the vehicle's warning buzzer chimed.

Frustrated, he turned and looked at the dash. He noticed the low tire pressure warning light was illuminated. Discouraged that he may have a tire in need of repair, he opened the car door and immediately walked toward the right front tire. A mere week prior the same tire was low and required air to be added.

He noticed the screw in the tread of the tire and pressed his hands against his hips. This was a risk he could not take. The tire would have to be repaired before he drove to the suburbs. Being stranded – today – was not an option. Not at all.

CHAPTER TWO

NEED A RIDE?

TWO. "Honey, don't forget your backpack," The mother reminded her six year old daughter as she ran into the kitchen.

Having a child in kindergarten was both a blessing and disappointment to Meghan. Living with her daughter for the last six years - watching her grow, seeing her learn, and anticipating her going to school had been rewarding. As the day approached for her to begin school, she dreaded the thought of her daughter leaving. The girl attending school had left the mother feeling alone and uncertain of her future.

Amanda attended school for a half day, yet those days had been the longest half days of Meghan's life. The complications with the pregnancy would prevent her from ever giving birth again. Those complications, combined with a few other things, attributed to the early ending of her marriage to Mark. She and Amanda now lived comfortably, but alone, spending half of Mark's inheritance.

She noticed that the girl's shoes were on the wrong feet. "Honey, your shoes."

Amanda looked down at the toes of her shoes and back up at her mother as if she had no idea of what was said.

She knelt down beside the young girl. "They're on the wrong feet, sweetie."

The little girl immediately sighed and dropped to the floor, grabbing her right shoe. Filled with frustration that she would disappoint her mother, she pulled the right shoe from her foot. As she did, her back pack fell to the floor.

"Sorry momma," the little girl half whispered as she struggled with her shoe.

"No, sweetie, it's okay. We can fix it, can't we?" Meghan asked.

As the little girl pushed her shoe onto her foot, she looked up and nodded at her mother. Struggling with the weight of her back pack, the girl stood, stumbled, and began to regain her footing. As she began to walk toward the entrance of the garage, she thought of the school projects she intended to bring home to her mother.

Meghan motioned toward the backpack. "Sweetie, what's in there?"

"Stuff," Amanda responded.

Meghan opened the rear door of the SUV. "We'll look in there when you get home today and see if we can lighten that thing up. It looks heavy. Sound good?"

She watched as the little girl nodded and climbed into the SUV. The stubborn *I'll do it myself* nature of children at this age was entertaining for the mother to witness. The mother turned away to keep from laughing as the daughter climbed up and over the seat, back pack in tow.

Looking at the reflection in the rearview mirror, Meghan admired her daughter's image. The similarities between the two were striking. The daughter was certainly an extension of the mother, and reflected her genes. The mother smiled a smile of pride as she started the SUV.

"Momma?"

"Yes, sweetie?" Meghan responded.

"Momma, why are butterflies so pretty, but crickets are so ugly?"

the little girl asked.

The mother coughed a laugh. "Well honey, let's see. God gives us all kinds of things on this earth, and some are beautiful and some aren't. But everything has a purpose."

"What about people? Brandon is ugly, momma," Amanda said.

"Oh baby. People can't help how they look. People are like butterflies and crickets, I suppose. Everyone has a place and a purpose. Everyone is beautiful in their own way." Meghan looked in the rearview mirror for a response, pursing her lips to keep from smiling.

Amanda turned and looked into the mirror, directly at her mother's reflection. "Momma, Brandon is uggggleeeee."

"Honey, Brandon can't help what he looks like. Do you understand? All people are beautiful in *some* way. I bet if you give Brandon a chance, you'll see that he's very nice," Meghan stated.

The little girl turned and stared out the window.

After a moment of silence, Meghan began to wonder the young girl's thoughts. She didn't like thinking of her hating anyone or not seeing the good that Brandon may have to offer. She broke the silence with the hope of persuasion. "Sweetie, have you tried to talk to him?"

Amanda turned from the window and looked into the mirror. "No, momma. He smells like peanut butter."

Meghan laughed out loud. The thought of someone smelling like peanut butter caused her to smile. As she continued to drive, she imagined a man of peanut butter odor asking her on a date. Pulling into the school entrance, she decided she would go on the date as long as the man was a true gentleman.

A true gentlemen with good taste.

Meghan parked and exited her door. As she opened the rear door of the vehicle, she noticed the young girl pulling against the restraints in the seat.

Meghan smiled. "Sweetie, just a minute, I'll unbuckle you. Are you anxious to get to school?"

Amanda nodded and grabbed her backpack as the mother unbuckled the car seat. As soon as the buckle was undone, Amanda began to slither between the door of the car and the mother's leg.

"Hey, come here. Give me a kiss," Meghan shouted as the young girl took off running toward the door.

As Amanda stood on her tip toes, the mother bent down to kiss her. "Your momma loves you, Amanda."

Amanda tugged on her overweight back pack. "Love you."

"Remember, everyone and everything has a purpose, okay?" Meghan said as her daughter walked away.

Amanda nodded a sharp exaggerated nod.

Meghan laughed. "Get going."

As Amanda turned and ran toward the school door, the mother wondered how she could ever go a day without seeing her. Next year would certainly be a challenge. Living in a small suburb had advantages, but nothing could shelter her from the fact that her only daughter was going to grow up.

Two more weeks of school, the summer, and Amanda would be gone. Meghan smiled as she watched Amanda pull the door open to walk into the school. As the young girl walked past the glass door, she turned and waved. That, standing alone, provided the mother all the reason in the world to smile.

And she did.

Meghan got into the car and drove along the paved drive away from the school. Driving into the sun, she noticed what was left of the now forgotten winter on the front of the car. The filth of a few snowstorms from early March made a mess of the city, and of her once clean Mercedes SUV. Now well on its way to May, the threat of snow was over. Meghan was prideful of her Mercedes; and the winter's grime made it look cheap and not unlike all of the other cars on the road.

Cleaning the car, relaxing with a cup of coffee, and an early lunch quickly became the plan to get the mother through the child's school day.

The secluded car wash was a departure from her typical route, but the car wash was a self-service type. Something about washing the car was satisfying to her - a form of reassurance that she didn't necessarily need a man in her life.

As she drove into the car wash, she was relieved that there were no lines. It should take her twenty minutes to wash the car, and then she could relax at the coffee shop for a good part of Amanda's school day. As she parked the car in the stall she reached for her purse.

As she sat in the stall, a white BMW sedan watched from the road that accessed the car wash. Calmly, the driver tapped his fingers on the steering wheel to the beat of the music. Somewhat impatient, the driver took a sip from his cup of coffee as the music continued to play.

As Meghan opened the door of her SUV and stepped into the wash bay, she thought of her daughter and smiled.

The driver placed his coffee back in the cup holder and inched forward toward the entrance.

As she fed her bills into the change machine, the white sedan inched toward the stall directly behind her. The driver smoothly turned the car in a semi-circle, and backed into the stall next to the vacuum machine.

15

The maneuver went unnoticed by the woman.

Ryan reached into his pocket and removed two quarters for the vacuum. As he stepped out of the car, he admired the tone of the woman's skin. This, to him, was his most important victim. This would allow the game to begin. The game would fuel him to continue, and the continuance would assure him of his calculating nature.

They were wrong about me, he thought as he placed the quarters in the machine.

As he began to vacuum the car, Meghan turned and faced him for a split second. Her smile caused him a brief moment's satisfaction. Satisfaction, in this form, was something that he cherished.

As she turned back toward the machine, he removed an eight-inch long piece of tape, handcuffs, and a Taser from the trunk. Fluidly, he approached Meghan from behind. As his hand cupped her mouth, he pulled one of her arms behind her back. With the tips of his fingers, he secured the tape over her mouth. The entire process took less than three seconds.

As he pulled her other hand to her back, he secured the loose handcuff. Swiftly, he picked her from her feet, and took three long steps to the trunk of the car. Carefully lowering her in the trunk, he pulled the vacuum hose and placed it back into the retainer beside the machine.

Ryan closed the trunk of the car and scanned the lot for any witnesses. Satisfied that there were no onlookers, he pushed his hands into the front pockets of his slacks, inhaled through his mouth, and grinned.

As he exhaled through his nose, his mouth twisted into a smirk. Content with his accomplishment, he pulled his hands from his pockets, opened the car door, and got in.

He buckled his seat belt, shifted the car into gear, and pulled from the lot. He drove away quite certain that there would be no one who could hear his new passenger. He had reinforced the trunk with sound deadening material and another inner layer of steel. The ten mile ride to his home would be unnerving to his new passenger, but would provide him no displeasure what so ever.

He removed his coffee cup from the cup holder and took a long drink. As he turned the music volume up, he pressed his index finger to his eye, against the lid. His eye twitching bothered him. To him, it was a sign of weakness. A sign of nerves. A sign of incompetence.

As he pressed his finger against his eye, his mind filled with wonder.

The thought of someone willingly forfeiting their life was fulfilling to him.

The real question was who?

Who would be *first*?

Incompetent?

Not in the least, he thought.

Not in the least.

CHAPTER THREE

QUADRUPLETS?

THREE. Confused and scared, Meghan pressed her feet against the inner walls of the trunk. The inner structure of the trunk, regardless of where she pressed her feet, was solid. She shifted her body and pressed her feet into the corners, attempting to kick out a taillight. Again the feeling of reinforcement discouraged her.

This obviously wasn't his first, she thought. Wonder filled her. *Why me? What does he plan to do? Will I ever see Amanda again?* The confusion turned to frustration and the frustration evolved into anger. She kicked harder.

And she began to cry.

She shifted to her side to relieve the pain in her arms. She had never been arrested, and at no time had ever been handcuffed. There was something about being bound that had always interested her, especially since her divorce from Mark. The darkness of the trunk began to sooth her. She closed her eyes, counted to three, and opened them again.

No difference.

She moved her arms, and found a position that was comfortable. As she attempted to pull her wrists apart, the metallic sound of the handcuffs reassured her that she not going to escape. She closed her eyes and became hypnotized by the repetitive sound of the car tires on the roadway beneath her.

Her thoughts moved from her current situation to her past. She began to think of her marriage, before Amanda was born. She and Mark were best friends that decided to marry. Based on their past experiences and love for each other, she had felt as if the marriage would last forever. She closed her eyes and recalled a time when they first moved in together as newlyweds.

They were having a talk about sex over breakfast. The home they had moved into was a in a nice neighborhood, and large enough for the family they had planned. The kitchen was large, and had an eating area at the end of the kitchen. Seated at the table, she had started a discussion with Mark about her sexual desires.

"Would you consider tying me up?" Meghan asked Mark.

"I guess I don't understand why," Mark responded with a look of confusion.

"I think it would be exciting," Meghan stated.

Mark chuckled. "Exciting? What about being tied up is exciting?"

"I think I would like it. When I think about it, it makes me wet, Mark. It excites me. I really don't know why," she explained.

"No, I don't think I'd like it. It's about what we *both* like, you know. What we want to share, right?"

After some consideration, she nodded.

"Anything else?" he asked.

She thought of Mark forcing himself on her, holding her down, and slapping her. The thought of it excited her greatly. She yearned to be taken, sexually. Forcefully assaulted, held down, called names, and slapped.

Against her will.

She knew, of course, she would be willing. The thought if her inner fantasies confused her. Since she was a teen, these thoughts were often recalled as she masturbated. The reason, to her, for the feeling of desire toward this forceful act was not clear. She rubbed her neck with her hand and responded.

She stood from her chair. "No, that's it."

"Don't get mad and leave," he said.

She turned her cereal bowl for him to see. "I'm not mad. I'm finished."

He narrowed his eyes. "Okay. I just don't want you getting mad over this. It creeps me out to think about choking you, holding you down, or slapping you."

"I understand. It was just a thought. You know, role play," she said.

He chuckled. "Put on a school girl skirt, that's role play."

The thought of it made bile rise in her throat. Thinking of grown men fucking school girls wasn't something that appealed to her. She stood at the sink and wondered why being raped or choked appealed to her so much. Frustrated, she rinsed her bowl and stepped from the sink.

"I'm going to go for a run," she said.

He extended his arm and stopped her in mid stride. "You're not disappointed?"

"No, not at all," she lied.

He puckered his lips in an exaggerated fashion. "Okay, kiss me."

She kissed his lips lightly and stepped around him. The disappointment was hard for her to hide. She wondered if she could live her entire life without having her true sexual wants, needs, desires, and fantasies fulfilled.

The rear of the car jolted, bringing Meghan from her relaxed daydreaming state. Although she opened her eyes, the darkness enveloped her. As the car jolted again, she blinked her eyes.

Speedbumps?

She shifted her weight on her hips, attempting to get more comfortable. As she twisted her torso, she realized she had become sexually aroused. Somewhat uncomfortable in her state of arousal, she twisted her hips, and attempted to roll onto her back.

Soaking. Wet.

As she felt the car turn a corner, she gritted her teeth and clenched her jaw. By her calculations, she had been in the car for fifteen minutes or so. The entire time, she had allowed herself to be filled with sexual thoughts, and not of her daughter. As the guilt began to build, she felt the car come to a stop.

The sound of her breathing filled the trunk. There was virtually no transference of outside noise into the trunk. As the car pulled forward, she blinked her eyes. She felt as if she could hear her heart beat.

Stopped again.

The vehicles engine was shut off.

She took a deep breath.

As she exhaled, the trunk opened. She squinted at the introduction of light to the trunk. She blinked several times and looked into the eyes of her captor. A handsome man in his late twenties or early thirties stood over her and smiled a soft smile. She shifted her weight, pushed against the trunk floor with her elbow, and sat upright.

"My name is Ryan Capshaw. I have no reservations in telling you this. You can think about why later. I'm going to remove you from the trunk, and I will do so carefully. Please, for your safety, don't resist. There's nowhere for you to go, and escaping is not an option."

He spoke very clearly and with a soft voice.

She blinked her eyes and lay still.

"I will not remove the tape from your mouth until we are at our destination. Additionally, I will place a hood over your head before I remove you from the trunk. If you are going to participate in your relocation favorably, please blink your eyes twice."

She blinked twice.

"To assure me that you understand, blink *once* again."

She blinked once.

He motioned toward the trunk with his index finger. "Most excellent. I'm going to cover your head now. The sitting up, that was impressive. Most are incapable."

As Ryan gestured toward the trunk Meghan noticed the watch on his wrist. For a moment she focused on his left hand and the watch that was on his wrist.

Most are incapable, she thought. This is not his first time doing this. She began to wonder about Amanda, and what she may be doing. The thought of her daughter being alone or with a stranger made her feel uneasy. She shifted her weight and looked up at Ryan. As his hand moved toward her head, she attempted to look at the face of his watch.

He pulled his arm from the trunk and squinted.

"The time? Are you concerned with the time? Or are you staring at something else?" he asked as he quickly pulled his hand from in front of her face.

She nodded.

"Interesting. Certainly." He rotated his wrist toward his face. "Ten thirty sharp. *Now*, are you ready?"

Meghan nodded again.

He placed the hood over her head. "Fabulous, here we go."

Once again, darkness enveloped her. Meghan's face now covered with the black hood, she could hear herself breathe. Each time she exhaled, the hot breath surrounded her face. Gently, his hands grasped her upper arms and began to pull her from the trunk.

He lifted her from the trunk. "I'm going to carry you for a moment, don't thrash around."

Meghan felt one arm around her shoulders and the other beneath her thighs. As he walked, she counted the steps.

Seven.

Stairs.

A door.

Twenty-two steps.

Another door.

Stairs.

Six steps.

He lowered her to the floor.

"Straighten your legs."

Something about Ryan's voice was calming. He spoke very clearly, concisely, and without hesitation in his voice.

As Meghan felt her feet touch the floor, she stood erect and straightened her shoulders. She felt his hands removing the hood. As the hood cleared her eyes, the dim light brightened the room enough for her to see.

Meghan heard faint voices in the rear of the room. Thoughts of what would be next began to fill her mind. As he folded the hood and placed it in his rear pocket, he looked at her and smiled.

"Loud noises tend to disturb me. I have faith that you'll be quiet."

Ryan removed the tape from her mouth in one swift pull.

Meghan looked around the large room and moved her lips freely, grateful that the tape had been removed.

He gestured toward her waist. "Turn for me, please. Face away from me."

Meghan turned around. She felt his chest against her back as his left hand tightened around her neck. She could feel his hot breath on her neck as her cuffed hands were pulled away from her back.

"I'm going to remove your hand cuffs now, and we'll have a short talk. Once again, I prefer this be without incident. Do you understand?" he breathed into her ear.

Meghan nodded.

The feeling of Ryan's hand on her neck relaxed her. As he reached for the cuffs, she exhaled and became limp against the hand around her neck.

As the handcuffs were removed, Meghan rotated her wrists, thankful for the freedom to move her arms freely again. A quick scan of the large room revealed nothing to her out of the ordinary. For all practical purposes, the room was empty. By her calculations and experiences it was approximately thirty feet wide and sixty feet long. Several doors were around the perimeter of the room, one of which was large and appeared to be steel.

Although Meghan could hear the voices beyond the steel door, she was unable to understand their conversations. As he released her throat from his grasp, she exhaled a sigh of disappointment.

Put your hand back, she thought.

She turned and looked at Ryan with eyes of wonder. As he began to speak, she focused on his eyes. An odd shade of grey with very long

25

eyelashes, she had never seen such eyes on a man.

"Inviting, aren't they?" Ryan asked.

"Excuse me?" Meghan muttered.

"My eyes. They're quite inviting," he responded.

Meghan blinked her eyes and nodded.

"You interest me, Meghan," he stated.

She smiled. The smile of pleasure quickly turned to curiosity. "You know my name?"

He stood before her with the handcuffs dangling from his right hand. "By all means. This was not a random abduction, Meghan. The details are not something I prefer to discuss, at least not now. I am going to explain some things to you. Listen carefully."

She nodded.

He placed the handcuffs in the rear pocket of his slacks. "I'm going to place you in a room with three other women. You're free to roam in the room. There is a bathroom, shower, toiletries, clothes, refrigerator, microwave, and music. Tomorrow, I will have additional instructions for you all. I want to make a few things extremely clear, are you paying attention?"

Meghan studied him as she spoke. She was five foot ten, tall for a woman. He appeared to be at least five or six inches taller, making him at least six foot two or three. He was very handsome, and appeared very well put together underneath his tan slacks and white dress shirt.

"Meghan, are you paying attention?"

His voice brought her back to the reality of the situation.

"Yes, I am. Sorry," she responded.

"Each of the women has been given the same instructions. If anyone attempts to harm me, overpower me, or escape, they will be killed immediately. The remaining women will all be killed after the attempted attack, one after another. Do you understand?" he asked.

Meghan attempted to swallow, but her dry throat prevented it. The dryness made her uncomfortable. She stared into his eyes and nodded.

"If anyone attempts to break anything in the room, or to fashion a weapon from any of the articles in the room, regardless of whether or not it is used against me in an attack, everyone in the room dies – one after another – beginning immediately following my awareness of something being broken. Do you understand?"

Oddly, Meghan felt calm. Considering the situation, she consciously thought of her lack of fear, and began to wonder if it would last. She blinked her eyes, studied Ryan's face, and forced herself to smile.

"Splendid. Tomorrow this will all begin to make some sense to you. I allow everyone one question, Meghan. You ask, and I will answer truthfully. This is not an invitation for an open discussion, but an opportunity to ask one question and have it answered. Think about what you're asking, and make certain it is something you want to know the answer to," he said in a soft monotone voice.

Meghan cleared her throat. "What is the address of this location?"

Ryan placed his index finger and thumb around his chin, cupping the palm of his hand against his jaw. He reached for her wrist, grasping it in his right hand. "Aren't you interesting? A thinker. I like that, Meghan."

The pressure of his grasp made her uncomfortable at first.

"Follow me," he instructed her.

The voices grew louder as they walked to the corner of the large room. As he approached the door, he held his left hand to a box on the wall beside the door. As his hand touched the box, a loud clicking noise came from the center of the door jamb. As he pressed against the door with his elbow, she felt his breath on her ear.

Ryan gently pushed her through the doorway and into the room. "616 Esthner," he whispered.

A loud metallic *clunk* from the door closing behind her reminded her of the permanency of her new dwelling.

Meghan blinked her eyes. As they became focused on the contents of well-lit room, she gasped. Shocked, she stood and stared at the three occupants of the room - each of which bore an almost identical resemblance of her.

CHAPTER FOUR

ONE OF YOU IS GOING TO DIE.

FOUR. "What's your name?" Dana asked as she stood up from the bench she was sitting on.

"Uhhm. I'm Meghan," she responded as she looked around the room.

As she noticed her hands begin to tremble, she clenched her fists in embarrassment.

Meghan quickly scanned the room. The room was square with concrete walls. A light in the center of the room provided the only illumination. A quick viewing of the room revealed no windows. A steel bench was built into the wall around three sides of the perimeter of the room. A door on her right was open, revealing what was obviously the bathroom. On the same wall as the bathroom door, a stainless steel refrigerator sat beside a steel shelf that housed a microwave.

The three women were all dressed in grey sweats, flip-flop style sandals, and white tank tops. The identical attire made a mental separation of the women difficult. Additionally, the all but identical physical appearance, hair color, and body structure made it almost impossible.

"Meghan?" Dana asked. "I'm Dana. Where you from?"

"Shut up, Dana," Elena said as she walked toward Meghan. "I'm in charge, remember?"

"I was just trying to be nice," Dana said softly as she walked back to the bench and sat down.

A third woman stood from the bench, sat, and stood again as Elena began to speak to Meghan. The woman began to make Meghan nervous. Fixated on the third woman, Meghan tried to comprehend the situation and focus on what Elena was saying.

Elena stood directly in front of Meghan and spoke with a slight hint of Spanish accent. "Where are you from?"

"Andover, I live in Andover," Meghan answered as she watched the third woman stand, sit and stand again.

Elena motioned to the woman now sitting on the bench. "Well, first things first. Introductions."

"That's Dana with the mouth," she stated as she motioned toward Dana, who was now seated on the bench with her head in her hands.

Elena looked up and down Meghan's frame. "The other one is Shellie. *The crazy one.* I'm Elena."

Meghan grinned and glanced at each of the women.

Elena pressed her hands against her hips and studied Meghan. "See, he's a fucking weirdo. I knew if he brought someone else, they'd look just like us. This is creepy as fuck."

"How tall are you?" Elena asked.

"I am uhhm. I'm," Meghan paused, shook her head, and attempted to process the question. The calmness of the women made her more uneasy than she felt she should have been. "I'm five ten."

"Jesus, we're all five ten. For once I wish I was five foot nothing. That fucking creep wouldn't have nabbed us if we were short. He has a hang up for tall brunettes with big boobs. And don't pay any attention to Shellie, she's fucking *loco*," Elena said as she turned toward the bathroom.

"I'll be right back, I gotta pee. We were all glued to the door when we heard the garage door open," Elena said over her shoulder as she stepped into the bathroom.

Shellie stood from the bench. "Did he tell you not to break anything?"

Meghan nodded. "Yes, he did."

"You dumb fuck. He told us all the same shit, Jesus," Elena screamed from the bathroom.

"Well, I'm just making sure. I don't want to die for some stupid reason," Shellie said apologetically.

"We're all going to die, you stupid bitch," Elena said flatly as she flushed the toilet.

Elena pulled her sweats up, washed her hands, and walked from the bathroom into the large open room. Frustrated with the amount of time she had been locked in the room, she often contemplated trying to escape. Thoughts of potentially returning home to her seventeen year old daughter were all that prevented her from attacking Ryan on one of the many occasions when he brought food or fresh clothes into the room.

"Do you ever hear of some fucking wacko kidnapping a bunch of girls and eventually they're set free? Or they escape? We've been through this - he's *planning* to kill us all. We should just figure out a way to get that door off the microwave and bust that *pendejo* in the *cabesa*," Elena said as she pointed to the microwave.

"English," Dana said from the bench.

"*We need to hit that asshole in the head*. He's going to kill us all. One at a fucking time. And we're all going to be as dead as bunch of dumb woman can be. Or, we can come up with a plan and beat this asshole and make a run for it. I'd much rather die trying to get out of here than after this prick fucks me and cuts off my hands," Elena said.

Meghan crossed her arms and pressed her hands into her armpits. "What do you mean about him cutting off our hands? He's going to cut off our hands?"

"I don't know what this fucker's gonna do. But that's what they *always* do. They cut of your *manos* and pull your teeth so you can't be identified. They always do that creepy shit," Elena's voice rose as she spoke.

"I think I am the last one." Meghan paused and looked around the room. "The last girl he was going to get."

"Why? Why you say that?" Elena asked as she scooted across the bench.

"He said tomorrow it will all start to make sense. Maybe he's bringing more people tomorrow, I don't know. I took it as tomorrow he was going to start something with us," Meghan said as she tried to recall exactly what Ryan had said.

Shellie stood from the bench. "Did he tell you his name?"

"Yes, Ryan Capshaw," Meghan admitted.

She said the name again - silently in her head. She liked the way it rolled off of her tongue when she said it out loud. Thinking of his hand on her neck, and how she felt when he whispered in her ear, she began to become uncomfortable with her feelings. Something about Ryan intrigued her. Truthfully, everything about Ryan intrigued her.

She guessed his age at late twenties, yet he drove a one hundred thousand dollar BMW sedan. He dressed well, and wore a Patek Philippe watch. Her father a jeweler, Meghan grew up with an understanding and a fondness for fine things, jewelry being no exception. She expected the watch Ryan wore cost $20,000 or more. She silently wondered what would cause a man of his stature and wealth to do such a thing to four women.

"He told us all the same shit, Shellie. Fucking stop with the stupid fucking questions," Elena said toward Shellie.

"Did he let each of you ask a question?" Meghan asked openly to the room.

"Fuck yes he did," Elena stated.

"Well?" Meghan asked.

Shellie sat down on the bench. "I asked if he was going to kill me."

"His answer?" Meghan paused, filled with wonder on what Shellie's response would be.

For some reason, Meghan felt as if she could trust Ryan. The feeling of trust troubled her, as she believed that naturally she shouldn't trust him. As Meghan recalled his eyes, his tone of voice, and his appearance, Shellie spoke.

Shellie's eyes fell to the floor. "He said, *that's my intent, yes.*"

"Why *me*? That's what I asked him," Dana blurted.

Meghan turned to face Dana.

"He said, *you're a piece of the puzzle,*" Dana continued.

Meghan thought of the question she had asked Ryan. If he was honest, it may come in useful at a later date. She hoped that it would come to that, and not the ending that all of the other women assumed to be imminent. Ryan was certainly making the rules. She began to wonder when he may touch her again, and when he did, what the circumstances would be surrounding the encounter. Her pleasure in Ryan's presence began to make her feel guilty.

"Fucking *puto*. I asked him when he was going to let me go. Dick-head said, *I have no intention of releasing you*," Elena growled as she moved to lie on the bench across from where Meghan stood.

Shellie began pacing the room. As she walked, she stared at the floor. Without looking up, she spoke. "What did *you* ask?"

"I asked how many more people were here," Meghan lied.

"What the fuck?" Elena barked as she sat up partially on the bench, "Why *that*?"

"I have no idea, it just came out. How long has each of you been here?" Meghan asked.

Shellie paced the room. "Two weeks, I think. I lost track. Maybe fifteen or sixteen days."

"Eight days," Dana responded.

Elena flattened herself out on the bench and stared at the ceiling. "I was first. I don't know how long I been here. Maybe three weeks - long enough that I know I am sick of it. I am ready to do *something*."

As Meghan turned and looked at each woman in the room, the resemblances between them struck her as odd. She contemplated the reasoning behind Ryan's choice of women, and what other similarities might not be as noticeable. As Meghan studied the women individually, Shellie continued to pace the room and stare at her feet.

"Is anyone married?" Meghan asked.

"No."

Nope."

Uhh. No."

"Well, neither am I," Meghan responded.

Meghan nodded toward each of the women. "Kids?"

"Yes, I have a daughter. She's seventeen, why?" Elena responded.

"I don't, no," Shellie responded as she continued to pace the floor.

"I don't have any children," Dana stated.

"Why you ask?" Elena asked.

Feeling as if she were assembling a puzzle, Meghan began to feel relieved. Almost instantly, the relief turned into grief. The thought of Amanda getting out of school started to worry her as she stood in the corner of the room. She realized, for all practical purposes, she hadn't moved since Ryan pushed her into the room.

She considered that she had no formal plan regarding her death concerning what Amanda's future would be beyond her death. Mark, by all means was excluded from her life, and never attempted to see Amanda. He had a legal *right* to see her, but he never exercised it. She wondered what the school would do – how long they'd wait before they started calling people.

Standing in the corner, her hands still under her armpits, Meghan tried to recall who she had put on the school's list of people to call in case of emergency. As she recalled that she had placed her mother on the list, she felt as if everything would be taken care of. As she thought of Amanda and the boy that smelled of peanut butter, her eyes began to swell with tears.

"What about you?" Elena asked.

Meghan wiped her eyes and responded. "I have a daughter. She's probably getting out of kindergarten now. She's six, her name is Amanda."

Elena patted the bench beside her with her hand. "It's okay, we all did it. Cry, get it out sister."

Meghan walked toward the bench on the wall to her left. "It's just. I don't know what's going to happen. I don't know where she'll end up – who will pick her up from school. She's going to be so scared. We were going to unpack her back pack tonight. She's really going to be confused."

Emotionless, Shellie continued to pace the floor. "We all have the same problems."

Elena motioned toward Shellie. "Don't pay attention to her, that's all she does."

Elena scooted across the bench toward where Meghan was beginning to sit.

"I don't have a living will, an attorney – anything. My husband hasn't really seen her since she was six months old. My *ex-husband* that is. I imagine she'll go to my parents. She's really going to have a tough time with this. Oh God. What has happened? *Why me?*" Meghan asked openly.

Megan placed her head in her hands and began to softly cry as Elena held her in her arms. Her head a whirlwind of emotion, she tried to remember if she locked the doors at her home before she took Amanda to school. She lifted her head from her hands and looked at the floor.

Meghan wiped the tears from her eyes. "My car. My SUV. It's at the car wash. It's unlocked and my purse is in the front seat. Fuckity fuck. My credit cards are in it. Perfect, this is just perfect."

Shellie looked up as she paced the floor. "Funny isn't it?"

"What's funny, weirdo?" Elena turned and asked, still sitting on the bench comforting Meghan.

Shellie stopped pacing. "What we think of when we first get here. After a week or so, it really doesn't matter. None of it will matter after he kills us. Where our purse is. Credit cards. Bullshit that doesn't matter. He grabbed me at the grocery store. I was worried about my milk spoiling."

Dana raised her head from the bench. "He grabbed me at the parking garage downtown. He's got my purse, I think. I don't know. Maybe he tossed it. I had it when he grabbed me. I paid three hundred and sixty dollars for that purse at the Coach store in the mall."

Meghan wiped her eyes on the back of her hand. "This is too much. I can't take this."

As she pushed Elena's hands from her shoulder she stood. She wanted Ryan to come back - talk to her - explain what he intended to do. She felt an odd comfort in his presence. When he was near her, talking to her, and looking at her, she felt as if other outside thoughts didn't enter her mind. When he was present, her brain didn't attempt to develop reason.

"Did anyone else talk to him very much?" Meghan asked.

"I talked to him for a minute or so before he put me in here," Dana responded.

"Did you find his voice soothing? Like hypnotic?" Meghan asked.

Shellie paced the floor, staring at her feet. "That's creepy to even ask,"

Dana looked up at the ceiling. "Yeah, I suppose. You know, when he spoke, I felt like I kinda *had* to listen. You know, like he was commanding me. But he really wasn't commanding. I don't know - it was just weird. I don't know how to explain it."

"He got me first. Probably why he talked to me for so fucking long." Elena chuckled. "He talked to me for a good ten minutes. Not really about anything, just told me he was going to lock me in this room. He went over his weird ass rules. He told me he was going to put more people in here. It was weird, I really wasn't scared."

Meghan looked around the room.

Shellie stopped pacing and turned toward Elena and Meghan, both now standing at the edge of the room by the entrance.

"Yeah, I thought about what if he raped me. Or whatever. Actually, I was *convinced* he was going to rape me. When he was driving, I kept thinking, any minute, this weirdo is going to pull over and yank me out of this trunk and rape me. It's weird, but I was sure *if* he did that, I could let him just do it – if he'd let me go. I had even decided if he *did* rape me, I wouldn't even tell anyone. I'd just keep it to myself and act like it never happened." Shellie began pacing after she completed her last spoken word.

Dana stood from the bench. "It's funny. You spend your entire life thinking if someone tried to rape you, how you'd dig his eyes out or kick him in the nuts. Then, someone nabs you, and you really start to think about it. Or, well I don't know. I didn't ever really think, *hey I'd like this guy to fuck me* while I was in the trunk. But I don't know, thinking about it *now*? Now I'm wishing he'd have fucked me and I would have run screaming into the woods or whatever. I'd trade that for this shit any day."

Dana finished speaking and began walking toward the bathroom. She opened the refrigerator door. "Anyone want a bottle of water?"

Meghan alternated glances between Elena and Dana. "There's water?"

Shellie stopped pacing and stared at her feet. "Oh. Yeah. He keeps us stocked up on stuff. He's just weird about the trash. We have to give him the trash."

Shellie began pacing again.

"I'll have one, thank you," Meghan said.

Dana handed Meghan a bottle of water, removed another, and closed the door of the refrigerator. Meghan removed the lid and tipped the bottle toward her lips. As she drank the water, she looked around the room at each of the women.

Megan sipped the water and recalled how she felt as she was secured with the hand cuffs in the trunk of the car. Being bound, the excitement of unknown, the stranger having all of the power over her had aroused her. Thinking of it made her feel excited again, but she was certain she shouldn't divulge her fantasies to the other women.

Meghan lowered the bottle of water from her lips. "So what's the deal with the sweats?"

"Oh, in the bathroom there's a cabinet. It has sweats, shirts and panties. There's electric razors, deodorant. There's pretty much everything you need in there. He picks up the dirty laundry, fucking weirdo," Elena responded.

"So, why do you suppose he chose us? Obviously, it wasn't *random*. We look like quadruplets. It's almost scary how much we look alike. And we're all divorced, two without children, and two with one daughter. It just seems weird. There may be more to this, I don't know. Probably just some weird kink of his. Where is everyone from?" Meghan asked.

"Wichita," Elena responded.

Shellie continued to pace the floor. "Augusta."

Dana sat down, took a drink of her water and placed the bottle on the bench beside her. "I'm from El Dorado. Weird, we're all about thirty miles from each other. I wonder if he wanted someone from each city or if there's something else to it."

"You're fucking stupid, Dana. He just *nabbed* us. It was random," Elena said.

Meghan sat down on the bench beside Elena. "No, that's impossible.

He was watching us. He knew my name. He called me by my first name when he got me out of the trunk. If I remember correctly, he said he had been watching me. I don't remember, he said *something* like that."

"Well, there's got to be something. I don't know now that it will do any good to know, but there has to be some way that he found us, something that we all have done or have in common or something."

Meghan took another drink of her water and thought.

Shellie stopped pacing. "Facebook?"

Immediately after speaking, she started pacing again.

"I don't have Facebook," Meghan stated flatly.

"But yeah. Some form of social media maybe. Maybe he picked us all off of the internet or something. He'd have to look a long time to find us by just wandering around. I mean hell, look at us, it's like looking in the mirror," Elena explained.

A sharp metallic sound came from the entrance door. In unison, each person turned to face the door.

The door opened.

"Ladies. I *was* going to wait until morning - but I must admit - I'm overcome with excitement. I have an announcement to make. Shellie, stop pacing please," Ryan said through the half-open doorway.

Each of the women were now standing and facing the doorway. Without thinking, and using her free hand, Meghan pressed her fingertips to her scalp and ran her fingers through her hair, flipping it over her shoulders as it fell from her fingertips.

She stood filled with wonder and an ounce of desire. She wanted to know what the future held, what may happen, and whether or not she would be allowed to live through this degree of captivity. Ultimately, she stood and stared at Ryan with a mind full of lust. She wondered what the other women thought about him – if his mere presence caused them want, desire, or lust. As she watched him stand in the doorway, she felt herself begin to tingle. She was beginning to become aroused. Consciously she questioned if he had any way of knowing her desires.

"Meghan, are you paying attention?"

The monotone note of Ryan's voice caught her off guard and caused her to stand erect and respond. She clutched her bottle of water with both hands. "Yes. Yes, Sir."

"Good, I need to make certain all participants are listening," he stated.

Participants? We're participants? In what? Meghan thought.

"As I stated a moment ago, it was my intention to make this announcement tomorrow, but I am incapable of waiting. So, listen carefully," Ryan demanded.

He inhaled through his nose, hesitated, and studied the group.

"Tomorrow at precisely zero-eight-hundred hours one of you is going to die."

CHAPTER FIVE

LIKE FATHER LIKE SON.

FIVE. "Glenfiddich eighteen, make it a double. Neat."

The bartender pulled the scotch from the top shelf. "You've got it Ryan, special occasion?"

A fixture at the bar, Pete had worked as a bartender at this establishment for twenty-one years. He admired Ryan. It wasn't often that someone ordered eighteen-year-old Glenfiddich. At twenty dollars a shot, it wasn't something most people would drink, especially someone as young as Ryan. Ryan had been patronizing the bar since his early twenties, frequently when he was home from college. After his completion of college, he generally stopped in nightly for one beer and simple conversation.

"Not so much, just a rewarding day," Ryan responded with a smile.

Ryan sat at the bar with his hands on his thighs, waiting for his scotch. Proud of his efforts for the day, he was eager to go to the next step with the women. The thought of them going through the process to decide who must die excited him greatly. The thought of it, to him, was arousing in a non-sexual way. It was an affirmation of sorts to his mental competence. As the bartender poured, he wondered who would be first to relinquish their life.

The bartender slid the scotch across the bar. "Investments go well for you today?"

Admiringly, the bartender looked over Ryan's choice of attire. Light wool slacks, a pressed light blue shirt, and the trademark Patek Philippe watch he generally wore were a testament to his hard work. The watch alone, the bartender knew, would cost $15,000.

Ryan raised his glass. "I'll let you know tomorrow, I suspect really well. Here's to being dedicated to our work."

Ryan thought of the four years he spent in college, and the seven years he spent in graduate school in Arizona. Obtaining a degree to be a Criminal Psychologist was not an easy task. Having a doctorate was an accomplishment in itself. The decision by the police force to declare him mentally incapable of holding the position of his dreams was inaccurate, inconsistent with his behavioral patterns, and a crushing blow to his feeling of self-worth.

As Ryan tipped the glass to his mouth the aroma caused him to salivate. His mouth continued watering as he began to take a sip of the scotch; the distinct odor reminded him of his father. *Like father, like son.* He had always despised that saying, and every time it came to mind, his jaw tightened. Sharply, he shook his head, clearing his mind of thoughts of his father. He pressed the glass to his lips and swallowed a mouthful of the single malt scotch.

"Well?" the bartender asked as Ryan lowered the glass from his mouth.

Although more than ten years his senior, the bartender admired Ryan's character, his manners, and his consistency. Years of bartending had exposed him to all walks of life – a good percentage of which were alcoholics. Ryan's one drink a night pattern was something the bartender wished that more people could adhere to. As Ryan smiled, the bartender

44

waited for his response.

Ryan placed the glass of scotch on the bar. "Aaaahhh. To describe this as calming would be a grotesque understatement. One drink is equal to two weeks of vacation."

"I admire your taste, Ryan. Shit, you could drink whatever you wanted wherever you wanted to. Hell, you come in here to my little shit-hole and drink. Been coming in here for a little bit, too." The bartender admired the watch Ryan was wearing. "New watch?"

Ryan smiled a prideful smile and raised his left hand from the bar, extending it under the watchful eye of the bartender. Since his denial of the position as a Criminal Psychologist he had been extremely fortunate with a few post sub-prime lending financial decisions, netting him hundreds of thousands of dollars profit. This earned profit was reinvested into stocks and other investments that performed equally as well. Ryan knew that his compulsive personality and intelligence made him a natural investor.

Ryan turned his wrist toward the light that dangled over the bar. "As a matter of fact it is. Do you like it?"

"Do I like it? Shit, you know I *love* watches. You have a weakness for money, I have a weakness for watches. That damn thing is gorgeous. Patek Philippe, huh?" Pete asked.

"Good eye, Pete. Yes it's a Patek. I got this one last week. Today is the first day I've worn it. I purchased it twenty-three days ago," Ryan stated, recalling the day that he abducted Elena.

"Don't struggle," he had told her as she began to kick her legs.

She continued to kick and attempt to free herself from his grasp. He shifted his right forearm in front of her neck, gripped his left wrist, and rolled his shoulder into the base of her skull, forcing her neck into his forearm. The process took less than five seconds, and she was unconscious.

He placed her limp body into the trunk, frustrated that she didn't listen. Things could have been so simple, but she chose to fight. The other girls all complied, but Elena was a fighter.

When he removed the handcuffs, she attempted to flee, requiring him to use the Taser to subdue her. As he had placed her into the room, he imagined she would be the last of the four victims to forfeit her life. Shellie, by his calculations, would be first.

Dana should be second, as she would be persuaded by the two stronger women – Elena and Meghan. Determining which of the remaining two would be next was a more difficult decision. Elena was more of a fighter, but Meghan had determination. As he lifted his scotch to his lips, he thought of what they may be discussing.

For a person to willfully give up living would be difficult if not close to impossible. Naturally, a person will try to survive under any or all circumstances – it is human nature. People with extremely low self-esteem, however, can be persuaded by a much stronger person to do what would normally be out of range for them to do – if left to their own devices.

He had no doubts, based on Shellie's test results, that she would be the first. By his best means of understanding, Dana would be second. After the first two were gone, the remaining two participants would certainly provide the most rewarding of revelations.

Pete wiped the water spots from one of the beer glasses. "So, you say you don't know if you did good or bad today?"

Pete's voice brought Ryan from his deep thoughtful state. The aroma from the scotch widened his eyes. He blinked and looked up at the bartender.

He nodded his head and finished the scotch in his glass. "I'm just not certain yet, Pete. I suspect tomorrow will be the beginning of some very rewarding days."

Pete placed the now spotless beer glass on the shelf behind him. "Got something big in the works?"

Ryan stood. "Huge."

Pete smiled as he turned around to face Ryan. "Fuck yes. That's what I'm talking about. Self-made millionaire in no time, I know you will."

Ryan stretched and turned toward the door.

"Leaving, bud?" Pete asked.

Ryan smiled as he removed a fifty-dollar bill and placed it under his empty scotch glass. "Tomorrow's going to be a big day, I need my sleep."

"Change?" Pete asked politely.

"You know better, but thanks for asking. I'm certain I'll see you tomorrow. Be well, Pete."

Pete waved as Ryan began walking toward the door. "Tomorrow."

As Ryan stepped to the door, he drew a deep slow breath, filling his lungs with stale aroma of the bar. The smell of the bar reminded him of his mother's basement. The smell of his mother's basement reminded him of his father. The thought of his father provided him all of the fuel, desire, and determination he needed to succeed.

He took another deep breath, exhaled, and opened the door.

CHAPTER SIX

I'LL DIE FIRST.

SIX. "Holy fuck. Holy fucking fuck." Elena turned, faced the bathroom door and pressed her palms into her thighs.

Shellie flopped onto the seat opposite the bathroom wall. "I'm going to throw up."

Dana sat on the bench beside where Meghan was standing and began to cry.

"Throw up then you raggedy assed bitch. I can tell you one fucking thing - I am not going to be that person. *Fuck that.* I am *not* going to be that person, so don't even ask. Anybody asks me, I'll choke you to death in your sleep," Elena barked.

Filled with emotion, Elena's breathing became labored. As she felt a lump rise in her throat, she attempted to swallow. After two failed attempts at swallowing, the bile began to rise in her throat again. As she took the two steps toward the refrigerator, she attempted to recall exactly what Ryan had said.

Tomorrow at precisely zero eight hundred hours one of you is going to die.

I will require that someone forfeit their life, willfully. This will allow the remaining women to live. If, when I return at zero eight hundred hours, no one is willing to forfeit their life, I will kill everyone in the room immediately.

Discuss this amongst yourselves and reach a decision.

The dark stain on the floor beneath the epoxy coating is an indication of what I am willing to do.

Sleep well.

Elena took a drink of her water and looked at the floor. A large stain underneath the grey enamel coating was almost as large as the room itself. In the three weeks that she had been in the room, she had not noticed the stain. Now that it had been brought to her attention, she couldn't bring herself to stop looking at it.

"Elena, you can't say that," Meghan said softly.

"I just did. And I'll say it again. Go ahead, one of you fuckers ask me, go ahead." She tipped the bottle of water to her lips and choked down another drink.

"That's what I thought," Elena added.

As she spoke, her stomach heaved, and the water rose in her throat.

Quickly, Elena turned, ran to the bathroom and leaned over the toilet. As soon as her head was over the stool, she began to vomit. As she vomited, she began to cry. The sounds of Dana and Elena crying filled the room. As she hovered over the toilet, she thought of her daughter. She would be the first of Elena's family to graduate high school. The graduation, if Elena's perception of time was correct, should be in two weeks.

Satisfied that she was done vomiting, Elena stood and walked to the sink. She rinsed her face and hands in the sink and looked up into the mirror. As she turned back toward the room, she shook her head in a combination of wonder and disgust.

"This sick fuck. How are we going to do this?" Elena asked as she walked into the room.

Dana sobbed as she looked up from the bench. "Draw straws?"

"We don't have any straws, and we ain't drawing straws. It's one of you three," Elena hissed.

"You can't say that Elena. You aren't *excluded*," Meghan responded.

"I just said it. He said *voluntarily*. I will never *volunteer* to have this sick piece of shit fuck me, kill me, or whatever he's gonna do. He'll probably cut us into little bitty pieces and spread us all over the city," Elena complained.

"Okay, fuck it. I'll just decide. Shellie, it's you. I hate you anyway. All you do is pace across the floor and whine. You bring Dana and me down. You're fucking annoying. It's you. There, it's decided," Elena growled.

"Elena!" Meghan screamed. "You can't do that. Basically, you're killing her."

Elena walked around the perimeter of the room. "I don't know her. And fuck you, too. I don't know *you*, either. Fuck that bitch, she can either agree to do it, or I'll just choke her out and toss her at him when he unlocks the door tomorrow."

The sound of Dana crying became louder.

Elena's remarks made Meghan uneasy. To be so willing to take the life of another human being made Elena no more sane or civil than Ryan. For a moment, Meghan pondered death, and what life meant to her. Thoughts of her daughter growing up without a mother began to trouble her. She thought of her sister, and whether or not she would volunteer to raise Amanda.

Meghan wondered the effect not having a paternal parent would have on her daughter as an adult. What effect, if any, her mother being murdered would have on her ability to live a productive life. She wondered how many people would come to her funeral, and if the service would be pleasant. She struggled with the thought of whether or not Mark would come to the service.

"I don't want to die," Shellie said.

"I'm not *going* to die," Elena said in a stern tone.

"How are we going to do this?" Meghan asked openly to the room.

Sitting on the bench, her elbows on her thighs and her face in her hands, Dana's sobs grew louder.

"I don't have…" Dana struggled to speak. "I don't have a family."

Tears ran down her cheeks. "I don't have any idea of how long I may live, and both my parents are dead."

She began to sob hysterically. "I can't…do"

"I can't…"

"I can't leave him alone."

Elena turned and faced Dana with a look of disgust. "I thought you said you were divorced."

With her eyes fixed on Dana, Elena shook her head. "You did. I know you did. You lying bitch you said you were divorced."

As tension filled the room the severity of the situation weighed heavily on Meghan's mind. She realized if she wanted to live, she would need to convince someone else to die. Fifteen minutes prior, the thought of doing so was nothing less than murder. Now, as she stood and watched Elena glare at Dana, the thought of persuading one of the others to die seemed to be nothing more than survival.

Preservation of her daughter's future.

Saving herself.

Preservation of *her* life.

Meghan looked at Shellie. Emotionless, Shellie sat on the bench and bit her fingernails. Consciously, Meghan decided that she agreed with Elena, Shellie needed to volunteer to die. Meghan would need to determine a way to convince her.

Elena stood over Dana, peering down at her. "I fucking hate liars. You lying bitch."

"Elena," Meghan whispered.

Elena turned to face her. Without speaking, Meghan shook her head and motioned to the floor beside her. Quietly, Elena approached Meghan. As she stood beside her, Meghan whispered into Elena's ear.

"We have to convince one of these two to do it," Meghan whispered.

"What…"

"What are…"

"What are you two talking…" Dana looked up from her hands and sobbed. "About?"

"We ain't talking to you, you lying bitch," Elena barked.

"Don't be so mean to her," Meghan whispered. "Let's be nice and see if we can talk one of them into it."

Elena nodded and took a sip from the bottle of water. Meghan tapped her on the shoulder, turned, and walked softly to the bench beside Shellie.

Meghan sat on the bench beside Shellie. "Let's talk about this sensibly."

Meghan turned to Shellie. "You live in Augusta?"

Shellie looked up from biting her fingernails and nodded.

"What do you do? For work?" Meghan asked softly.

Shellie nibbled at her nails. "I drive a bus. A school bus."

Without expressing emotion, Meghan began to consider how to approach Shellie regarding death. As Meghan thought of what to say, she realized that not one material thing she owned was as valuable as life. It seemed ridiculous of her to even try to reason with coming to terms with death. Nothing was more valuable than life, and there was not one thing anyone could say to her would convince her otherwise.

"So, you're divorced?" Meghan asked quietly.

Shellie nodded.

"What do you make driving a bus? Thirty grand?" Meghan asked.

Shellie turned to Meghan and smiled. "Thirty-four."

Meghan nodded. As she looked up at Elena, Elena smiled and walked toward Dana, who continued to sob into her hands.

Elena sat on the bench beside Dana and put her arm over Dana's shoulder. As she did, Dana looked up. Her eyes swollen, and her face covered in tears, she attempted to speak.

"I have…" Dana pulled the bottom of her shirt to her face and wiped her tears. "I uhhm. I have. Oh God. This is so hard."

"I have breast cancer." As the words escaped Dana's mouth she became less controlled in her breathing and the sobbing slowed to an uncontrolled gasping for breath.

She wiped her eyes with the back of her hand and coughed as she tried to speak again. Elena offered her bottle of water to Dana. Dana looked up, accepted the bottle, and took a drink.

"I found out two months ago," Dana said. "It doesn't look good. My mother and my aunt have both…"

Elena took the bottle of water from Dana's hand and patted Dana's shoulder, comforting her. "I'm so sorry," Elena offered in a soft voice.

"I've been thinking about dying for two months, and I don't want to die." Dana sobbed onto Elena's shoulder.

"None of us do," Elena breathed. "It really doesn't look like we have a choice, it's just a matter of time."

Dana raised her head from Elena's shoulders and nodded. "I know, this is all so crazy. I've been two months fighting this and now it looks like it really doesn't matter. I suppose it's all God's will."

Elena shook her head. "God has nothing to do with this."

Dana wiped her forearm across her face. "Why would you say such a thing?"

"It's true. Look around you. God isn't here, Dana. If God were here, we'd be on a beach somewhere, or shopping. Or I'd be at my daughter's graduation. This is *El Diablo.*" Elena glanced around the room.

Dana fought to catch her breath. "God is always present."

Elena released Dana's head from her shoulder and stood from the bench. "No. No. No he isn't. Not *my* God. He isn't watching this shit and letting it happen. Sorry, *chica.*"

"*Your* God? Are you a Christian?" Dana stood from the bench as she spoke.

"Yes, I'm a Christian," Elena said over her shoulder.

Elena walked toward the door, thinking of her attendance at church as a child. Her family was raised Catholic, and as a child she attended church regularly. Her parents *required* that she attend church. It was part of her family's schedule of weekly requirements. Her family grew up close in Texas, close to poverty, and she had become pregnant at seventeen. The religious belief of her family and the church prohibited marrying outside of the religion, premarital sex, or the possibility of abortion.

Feeling trapped and alone, she left her family, moved to the midwest, and abandoned her religious beliefs. For the last seventeen years, she had lived with her daughter. Although she had boyfriends on and off, she had never been in an actual relationship with a man as a live-in partner or a husband.

Now, standing in the corner by the door, Elena began to wonder about her separation from God and church. She began to wonder if she were closer to God if this situation would potentially be different. She stared at the floor and tried to remember the last time she had attended church.

"And you don't think God has anything to do with this?" Dana asked.

"Shut up, Dana. I'm not going to talk about this anymore," Elena said sharply as she turned away from Dana and faced the opposite wall.

Dana wiped the remaining tears from her face. "Maybe it's what we all need to talk about."

"Bitch, you keep nagging at me, I'll make sure your dead ass is lying at this door in the morning," Elena barked as Dana approached.

Dana ran her hands through her hair and scratched her scalp with her fingertips. It was difficult for her to process someone claiming to be a Christian yet demanding God had no involvement or knowledge of events or happenings in their life. Raised in the mid-west, and a Methodist, Dana believed that God was forever present in her life.

"God is our refuge and our strength, a very present help in trouble. Psalm 46:1," Dana said softly.

Elena turned, raised her right arm, and punched Dana in the mouth. As soon as her fist made impact with Dana's face, Dana fell to the floor and began crying.

Meghan jumped from the bench. "Holy shit, Elena!"

"Oh my God," Dana said. She wiped her mouth and looked at the blood on the back of her hand.

"Yeah. See? *Your* God let you get your ass smacked, bitch. Keep it up. You'll be waiting by the door in the morning. In a fucking pile, *pendeja*," Elena shouted.

Meghan approached the two women. 'What the fuck?"

Elena spat on the floor beside Dana and took a step in the other direction. "Fucking bitch was God *this*, God *that*, *God, God, God*. I fucking told her. Bitch."

Meghan walked into the bathroom and returned quickly with a wet washcloth in her hand. Sitting upright and against the wall, Dana held her hand to her mouth. Meghan knelt beside her and handed her the washcloth.

Dana said as she accepted the washcloth. "Thank you."

She wiped her mouth and looked at the bloody washcloth. She shook her head and wiped her mouth again with the wet cloth. Now regretting her having mentioned God, the pressure she placed on Elena, and mentioning her religious faith entirely - she began to question her ability to remain in the room safely and peacefully. With a heart full of regret and sorrow, she attempted to stand. As she stood, her legs wobbled beneath her.

Meghan reached under Dana's arms to help her stand. "Here, let me help you."

"Fuck *that* bitch. Leave her ass on the floor," Elena shouted across the room.

Meghan shook her head as she held Dana upright.

"Thank you," Dana whispered.

Meghan blinked her eyes in acknowledgement.

Meghan alternated glances between Elena and Shellie. "I was just explaining to Shellie my reasoning in all of this. Trying to make the best sense of it."

"And?" Elena asked.

Meghan turned to face the bench that Shellie and Elena were sitting on. "Well, without a doubt, someone is going to have to volunteer tomorrow morning to die. If not, we *all* die. I think we have to look at both sides of all available options. Hear me out, okay?"

Shellie nodded and continued biting her fingernails.

"Whatever, okay," Elena sighed.

"Well there are really three scenarios. Correct me if I'm missing something." Meghan paused as she stood before the two seated women, with Dana standing immediately behind her. "He kills one person and stops, that's an option. And if he stops, he may keep the remaining people in here forever. That's one scenario. The second one is this - he kills us all one at a time. Either of those two options, really, are the same as dying. It just gets down to which one of us has the guts to be the first - but the end result is the same, pretty much. The last option - he stops after the first person agrees to die, and releases the remaining people."

Meghan glanced in the direction of each woman. "So, let's assume death or a life of captivity. None of us will ever see any of our friends, family, or anyone ever again. None of *this* really matters. Who's first, who's last, who has the guts or who doesn't. But, if *one* person dies, and the others live, we should consider this, as a group."

She drew a deep breath. "Whoever agrees to die? Whoever that person is, the rest of us must agree to take care of that person's daughter or family or whatever. Whoever doesn't die, whoever lives through this - they must be able, willing, and have the resources to take care of the deceased persons daughter. So, in my opinion, the least capable should consider going first. You know, in hopes of the rest of us, or at least *one*

58

of us living. And that living person or persons will care for the deceased person's family."

Meghan paused and waited for rebuttal.

"Sounds reasonable, I'm *very* capable," Dana said in a muffled tone from behind the washcloth that covered her mouth.

Elena shifted her weight on the bench. "Bitch, I am tired of that mouth. You're dying of breast cancer; you should be first."

Meghan turned and faced Dana. Dana pressed the washcloth tightly to her mouth and nodded. The small amount of sorrow Meghan felt for Dana was soon overcome with an intense feeling of relief that Dana was dying of cancer. Her imminent death, if left in the room for any period, would certainly make Dana a prime candidate for the first or potentially second victim. Meghan released a slow inaudible sigh of relief.

Meghan raised her right hand to her face and covered her mouth. "I'm sorry, Dana. I truly am," she lied.

She closed her eyes and attempted to appear to be stricken by grief.

Softly, Dana began to cry. She cried for reasons other than her cancerous breast. She stood knowing that once she begun to speak of God, she felt she had gained the strength to forfeit her life. She didn't like thinking of it, and naturally she fought the thought of dying altogether. She stood before the other women knowing that when the time came, she would be willing to give up her life to potentially save the lives of the rest of the group.

As Dana held the washcloth tight to her now swollen lip, she looked down at the floor, closed her eyes, and said a prayer for the group of women. She prayed again for the well-being of her family; and lastly, she prayed for Elena. She opened her eyes, raised her head, looked at the group, and softly spoke three words.

"I'll die first," Dana said without a tone of emotion in her voice.

CHAPTER SEVEN

STOP. FUCKING. CRYING.

SEVEN. Ryan picked up his bag and walked toward the stairs at the corner of the weight room. The daily exercise was something that he started as a late teen. The constant reassurance by his father that he would always be overweight, worthless, and unintelligent had driven him to alter his daily routine to include exercise and proper diet in his life.

The result was a six foot frame of one hundred and ninety pounds, all of which, by any account, was muscle. Ryan carried the bag down the steps and recalled his many trips up and down the stairs of the basement at his mother's home. The thought of his father made his jaw tighten as he hurried down the steps toward the exit of the gym. As he reached for the handle of the door, he drew a slow breath and thought of *the* day.

"You're a fat little fuck, look at yourself," his father had told him.

Eleven years old and naked, Ryan stood in front of the mirror that was fixed on the wall in the basement. As he looked into the mirror, he saw an overweight boy looking back at him. His mind filled with fear of what may be next regarding punishment, his legs began to shake.

"Do you have any suggestions, you ridiculous pile of blubber?" his father asked.

"None, Sir," he responded, trembling.

"You realize I do this because I love you, correct?" his father asked as he circled Ryan's body.

"Yes, Sir," Ryan responded.

"If I didn't care what your fat little ass weighed, I'd let you turn yourself into a human fucking beach ball. You're disgusting, Ryan. In fact, I can't even decide what to do with your fat little ass next. Nothing seems to motivate you," his father bellowed as he now stood in front of Ryan and stared at his slightly overweight frame.

His father paused and shook his head at the young boy. "Well, we have tried giving you enemas. That didn't work. You remained disgusting. We tried starving you, and somehow you found food - so that's out. I can't force you to exercise, I haven't got time."

"Lessons. Life is about learning lessons. The earlier in life we learn them the quicker we are able to make corrections to our lives. Does that make sense?" his father asked.

Ryan, now crying, nodded his head.

"And another thing. You're always crying about something down here. Every damned time we come down here, you cry about something. It makes me damned near as sick to hear you cry as it does to look at your disgusting fat little ass. Stop. Fucking. Crying," his father demanded as he stood before him with his hands on his hips.

Ryan bit his lower lip with his teeth in an attempt to stop sobbing. The attempt made the crying much worse.

His father held his left hand in the air and pointed up with his index finger. His hand was rock steady as he spoke. "Do you realize why I am as successful as I am?"

"No…"

"No, Sir," Ryan blubbered.

His father moved his index finger within inches of Ryan's face. The tip of the finger was missing, making the finger square at the tip. It had been that way as long as Ryan could recall. Ryan focused on the finger and wondered the significance.

"I can't stand to even look at you any longer. I think I may need to go upstairs and vomit. You disgust me. Thirty days, Ryan. Thirty days. We'll mark it on the calendar upstairs. You have thirty days to lose twenty pounds. If not, you'll be taught a lesson the hard way. I'm going upstairs. I don't want to see your fat little face again tonight. Sleep in the room down here. I'll tell your mother you're sick. Get dressed, you fat little bastard," his father turned and walked to the stairs.

As Ryan heard the basement door close, he picked up his clothes and got dressed. He spent the night as he spent many nights as a child. Alone and attempting to determine what he could do to earn his father's praise and love. Regardless of his lack of ability to lose the weight his father had demanded, this day was the day he would turn his life around.

As Ryan opened the trunk of the car and tossed in the gym bag he shook his head. The thought of his father made him tense. He had started his daily workout today a little earlier than normal - to relieve tension. As he got into the car he took another deep breath and exhaled.

He turned his left wrist and checked the time. The inexpensive digital Timex watch he wore to the gym confirmed he had forty-five minutes to drive home and prepare for the volunteer to forfeit her life.

As he started the car and backed out of the parking stall Ryan considered all of the options that may take place in the events of the morning. As he weighed each of the possibilities, he smiled. He was certain not many people on earth had ever put a plan in pace with such intricacies and potential rewards.

Even his father would be proud.

CHAPTER EIGHT

VOLUNTEERING TO DIE.

EIGHT. Ryan took a deep breath and pressed his left ring finger to the pad beside the door. As the magnetic lock unlocked, he pushed the door open and exhaled. The level of tension he felt was much more than he expected it to be. Excitedly, he opened the steel door and peered inside.

"Have we made a decision, I'll allow sixty seconds for the response." His voice echoed into the concrete room.

As three women cried, Dana stood from the bench. Surprised, Ryan waited for someone to speak. Slowly and methodically, Dana walked toward the door.

"Stop," Ryan said as she reached a distance of a few feet from the door.

He glared at the three ladies sitting on the respective benches opposite each other. "Is *this* the decision? Dana? *You're* the volunteer?"

Dana nodded without speaking.

He grinned. "*Interesting.* Please turn and place your hands behind your back, I am going to handcuff you, but I will attempt to make it as comfortable as I can, okay?"

Dana shuffled her feet in a circular motion and faced away from Ryan. As she placed her hands behind her back, Ryan affixed the handcuffs lightly to her wrists and pulled on the chain.

He motioned toward the door. "Step through the door, Dana."

As Dana walked through the door, Ryan placed his hand on her shoulder and looked into the room. The women, staring down at the floor, continued to cry. None faced the door or watched as Dana was handcuffed. As the women sobbed, Ryan interrupted.

"Ladies." Ryan paused and waited for them to look up. None did. "Ladies, *your attention please.*"

As the women looked up and toward the door, Ryan continued. "Tomorrow. Same time same rules. I need another volunteer. Have a fabulous day. Zero-eight-hundred. Let us not forget."

He pulled the door closed. A soon as the metallic sound of the lock clicked, he checked the door to ensure it was locked. After confirming the security of the door, he placed his hand on Dana's shoulder and escorted her to a room on the opposite side of the basement.

Once in the room, Ryan assisted Dana to a table located in the center of the room, and pulled out a chair.

He pulled the chair out from the table. "Please, have a seat."

He motioned toward the handcuffs. "Be careful with your arms, I know that can be uncomfortable."

He sat at a chair on the opposite side of the table. "Now, are you comfortable?"

Dana nodded and looked around the room.

"Oh my. Your lips? What happened to your lips?" he asked as he noticed Dana's swollen lips.

"I fell," Dana lied, not wanting to potentially cause grief for any of the other women in the room.

He shook his head from side to side. "I doubt that, but fine. Stick to that story for now."

"First, I have a question," he said. "up until this moment we have before us, what is one memory you wish you could remove from your memory bank? Only one."

Dana studied Ryan, took a slow breath and wondered. She contemplated her answer, and opted to be honest in her response.

She began to cry. "The memory of these events - and more specifically - the memory of having chosen to die. At that moment, the feeling...*the letting go*, it was excruciating."

He placed his chin in his hand and waited. "How did or does it feel? Explain in one sentence."

Dana again thought, considered what to say, and responded.

Tears ran down her cheeks. "I feel as though I am dead already."

"Very interesting. Certainly what one would assume, I suppose. Very interesting to know for certain. Let's get on with this, shall we?" Ryan asked as he reached for the remote control. "As you can see, there's a camera on the tripod beside me. The light will come on just about *now*."

He pressed the button on a remote control that sat on top of the table. A green light on the face of the camera illuminated. The camera was facing Dana's seat. As Ryan finished speaking, Dana looked up at the camera and back down toward Ryan. Ryan smiled, placed his elbows on the table, and his chin on his clenched fists.

Ryan raised his chin from his hands and waved his hand toward the items spread out on the table. "Alright, let's get down to the *brass tacks* as they say. This, as you may or may not have imagined - this is being recorded. I am going to give you several options. With each option, should you accept it, there will be other potential options associated with the decision you make. I am not trying to confuse you, and I realize you probably didn't sleep well - but I have taken that into account. Let's get started, shall we?"

On one side of the table, a small stack of cotton towels lay beside a surgical scalpel, gauze, rubbing alcohol, and medical tape. On the other side of the table, a large amount of cash was stacked in four piles of identical height. In the center of the table sat a purse and a wallet.

He reached for the wallet and opened it. He removed the driver's license, held it close to his face, and studied it. Satisfied, he held it in front of the camera for a few seconds before speaking.

"Can you state your name, please?" he asked.

"Dana." She coughed and cleared her throat. "Dana Mitchell."

"Very well. Thank you." He placed the driver's license back into the wallet, and dropped the wallet into the purse. "You have volunteered your life on this day, have you not?"

He shook his head, and continued. "Well, let me rephrase that. Strike the last question. You were advised last evening that someone had to die today, and you volunteered to be that person, is that correct?"

Dana nodded.

"Verbally acknowledge the question, please," He stated calmly.

"Yes, I did."

"Very well," he said. "I am going to explain some things to you today. They may or may not make sense, but I think you are owed some form of an explanation. Are you paying attention, Dana?"

She nervously shifted her weight in the chair. "Yes I am."

"Lessons. Life is about learning lessons. The earlier in life we learn them, the quicker we are able to make corrections to our lives. Does that make sense?" he asked.

With a confused look on her face, Dana nodded. She had anticipated coming out of the room as a volunteer, being shot, and her body being thrown in a ditch in the rural area surrounding the city. This question and answer session was troubling to her. She began to wonder if Ryan knew this, and was trying to cause her more grief than he already had. Mentally, she was losing touch with her willingness to die. As Ryan spoke, she began to pray.

"Very well. Alright," Ryan spread his hands out and motioned at the contents on the table.

"As you can see, we have quite an arrangement on the table in front of us. Let me explain, and please do not interrupt. Is that clear?"

"Yes it is," Dana said flatly.

"Very well. I am going to explain a few things first." He inhaled a deep breath. "Plenty of Fish. The dating website. You have or shall I say *had* an account there. You filled out a questionnaire on that site for your profile. It had a few hundred questions. The responses to those questions placed you in several categories that allowed me to carefully pick you from a list of tens of thousands of potential candidates. I was able to separate you by height, hair color, and even your personality and income level. It made the selection of you four candidates very easy. All of you, in physical resemblance, were identical. In personality and level of wealth and upbringing, all so very different."

Dana sighed, became somewhat embarrassed, and slumped a little into her seat. She wasn't sure why at this juncture, and for what reason, but she felt guilt from Ryan finding her on the dating web site. She sat and watched him speaking, realizing that something about him caused her to admire him. She wasn't able to decide if it was his handsome looks, his means of dress, his expressed wealth, or his very matter of fact personality. As Ryan began to speak again, she shook her head lightly and dismissed it as a form of attachment to her abductor she had no conscious control over.

He grinned. "You know; I wonder what people think when they fill out those questionnaires. It reveals a considerable amount about a person. It lets people like me hand pick a candidate to fit into a certain slot. I could have told you that either you or Shellie would be the first volunteers. Let me guess, you decided to volunteer because of your closeness to God. Am I right?"

"Yes, I guess so," she responded.

He smiled and placed his palms on either side of his face. "Exceptional. This is such fun."

"Well, let's get to the meat of this lesson. Do you understand the risks associated with the use of such websites, and the things that you divulge when you fill out such questionnaires?" he asked.

Her eyes fell to the table. "Yes, I suppose so."

"You're extremely calm, this is easier than I expected. You must have a great relationship with God, but I am not going to get into that right now. Options. Let's go over options." He snapped his fingers sharply. "Are you paying attention?"

"Yes. Yes, I am paying attention," she responded

"To live or to die. Choices and lessons. Alright. Here's the biggie as they say. I will allow you to choose to live; but if you do, I must disfigure you. I will take the scalpel and remove a portion of your body, and I will not tell you in advance what portion it will be. It will, however, be limited to one portion of your body, not *multiple* pieces. And, as I have no anesthetic, it will be painful. You will, I am quite certain, remember the event if you so choose this option, and learn a valuable lesson. *Oh my*, that sounded bad, didn't it?"

As Dana sat and thought of what Ryan had offered, she began to think of being cut with the scalpel, and the pain associated with the procedure. First, she imagined him cutting off her nose, and what she would look like for the rest of her life without a nose. She imagined her foot being removed and the pain that would develop as he attempted to cut the skin and flesh around her foot. She contemplated the amount of time it may take, and how much blood loss there would be as he cut around the circumference of her ankle. She wondered for a moment what he would do to sever the bone after he removed her foot. She imagined that she may bleed to death if he tried to remove an entire limb. Slowly, she looked over the table for sutures and a needle, and saw none.

Dana felt her stomach convulse and fought to swallow.

Ryan sat back in his chair and covered his mouth. "Oh please, don't *vomit*. Let's not start that. The floor is concrete, but still, let's just *not*,"

"Well, think on that for a moment. The other option is this. You will die an almost painless death, and I will donate the stack of money on my left to whichever family member you choose to be the recipient. I assure you as a man of my word, should you choose the latter option - the money will be donated without reservation."

He waved in the direction of the pile of money.

Dana coughed, swallowed, and looked at the pile of money. She contemplated what type of life her family could live with the money, and how they may evolve differently without having her as a family member. The money certainly wouldn't solve *all* problems, but it would prevent many. She blinked her eyes, looked down at the table, and thought of living without a nose, hand, or possibly an arm.

She blinked again and thought of her cancer. What if she were fated, in God's eyes, to die anyway? She didn't know the answer, and never would. She stared at the pile of money and tried to remember her days as a teller at the bank when she was 21 years old. Her best recollection was that there was a thousand dollars in a banded stack of one hundred dollar bills. She attempted to calculate the amount of money stacked on the table. She blinked her eyes again and lost track of the stacks she had counted. Frustrated and confused, she looked up and toward Ryan.

She nodded toward the money. "How much money is there?"

"Five hundred thousand dollars," he responded sharply.

She shifted her weight in the seat and rotated her shoulders in an effort to get comfortable. She looked at the money, turned and looked at the scalpel, and then at Ryan. Calmly, she looked down at her lap, closed her eyes, and began to pray.

She opened her eyes. "I'll allow you to disfigure me."

He rubbed his hands together. "Interesting. Are you certain?"

"Quite," she responded without emotion.

He stood from his chair and reached for the stack of towels. "Outstanding."

He picked a towel from the stack, unfolded it, and placed it in the center of the table. Slowly, he walked around the table and stood behind the chair that Dana sat in. "Lean forward, please. And by all means, don't try to escape, agreed?"

"I won't," she assured him.

He reached behind her and unlocked the handcuffs. Carefully he removed them from her wrists, and placed them on the table beside where she was seated. As he walked toward his seat she raised her hands to the table and rubbed her wrists.

He sat down in his chair. "I actually prefer not to use the handcuffs to be quite honest. I just feel I need to use *something*. You know, to deter any kind of bad decisions on your part. And I'm not implying you would attempt anything, it's just best for both of us. Well, you understand, don't you?"

She attempted to rub the pain from her wrists. "Yes I do."

"And, I don't want you to think for one minute that this entire thing has been about teaching you a lesson about internet dating sites. It's much deeper than that. I wouldn't gather up four identical women and mentally torture them to teach them a lesson about safe dating. I'm not *completely* mad. To me, it's well…"

He coughed a laugh, covered his mouth with his hand, and continued. "It's about money. It's about success. Ultimately, I had to find four particular women. To find you in the typical public setting would have taken a lifetime. It may not even be something I could have done in *two* lifetimes. I don't know, Dana. But I know this; having that dating website with the profiles and photographs – that saved tremendous trouble, and has made this venture very profitable."

Her face washed with wonder. "So, someone is paying you to do this?"

"Oh no, quite the contrary. I devised the plan. The game. The entire thing. I developed it myself." Feeling prideful from his accomplishments, Ryan rubbed his hands together and paused from speaking.

"Game? This is a *game*?" Dana asked.

"Well, it's difficult to explain. Yes, a game of *sorts*. I maintain an interest in psychology, and the human mind in general. Sexually speaking, the wilder the desire, the more thought-provoking I find it. Not necessarily for me, so to speak - just stimulating *in general*. The gentlemen that spend time in the BDSM lifestyle range from interesting to downright scary. While reading profiles and postings on Fetlife's website - for entertainment purposed only, I might add - I encountered multiple wealthy Japanese business men that possessed certain kinks. One thing led to another, and I developed this *game*. It's similar to betting on a horse race." Proudly, Ryan pointed toward the camera. "See, the camera for instance. It's recording data that is being fed to a hosting site that provides live private streaming to the partners who have invested in the game. We have all placed multiple wagers regarding who would be first to volunteer, and which option, ultimately, the person would choose. You could have chosen death, disfigurement, or any other number of options. Had you picked death, I would have given you other options – including the manner in which you chose to die. All of these potential options have odds placed on them."

"The house, that's *me*." He motioned to himself. "Covers the odds."

Dana covered her mouth with her hand, feeling ill from her understanding of what was happening. A game with four the women - and lives being forfeited for money made her ill. For some reason, a random act of violence was far more acceptable. She thanked God for the ability to choose life, and hoped Ryan was a man of his word. She prayed for the strength to be able to endure the pain associated with the torture that Ryan was preparing to expose her to.

"Dana?" Ryan snapped his finger loudly. "Did I lose you?"

"No, I am listening," she murmured.

He waved toward the pile of money. "You appeared to have faded away. I thought maybe the injury to your face. Well, never mind. As long as you're paying attention, that's all that matters. Now, one last time, are you certain you choose disfigurement over death?"

She wondered for a split second where precisely Ryan had bet his money. Giving her the options again, she assumed his money was bet on her death. She found a small amount of comfort in thinking that she may be causing him to lose money in his sickening wager.

She stared down at the scalpel. "Yes, I am certain."

He stood and smiled a soft smile. "Very well,"

Ryan reached into his right pocket of his slacks and removed a pair of rubber gloves. As he pulled them onto his hands, he tightened his jaw and clenched his teeth. Memories of his father began to fill his head. He looked up from his hands, and focused on the pile of money. As he walked around the table, he picked up one of the towels from the stack.

He walked around the table and stood beside Dana's chair.

He handed the small folded towel to Dana. "Here, you'll want to bite on this. It'll prevent you from screaming, and provide some assurance you will not bite your tongue."

She accepted the towel and swallowed the bile that rose in her throat. She prayed again for God to give her strength. As Ryan began to speak, she closed her eyes and said a prayer asking God's forgiveness for what Ryan prepared to do to her. She opened her eyes and looked up at Ryan.

"I'm ready," she said as she placed the towel in her mouth and bit down on it.

"Well, we both know I could make this as torturous or as simple as possible. You've proven to be an extremely strong woman. This part isn't really for any reason, it's just. Oh, well, it's just that I have to do *something*," Ryan stated as he leaned over and picked up the scalpel.

"Place your left hand on the towel in front of you and fan out your fingers. Pick up the other towel in your right hand and hold it," Ryan inhaled a slow breath, looked up at the light fixture and exhaled.

As Ryan looked back down toward Dana's hand he began to speak.

"I'm going to cut off the very tip, just a small amount, mind you – of your left index finger. I'll have you know, it really won't hurt much at all. I won't remove much, and I'll make it as quick as possible. As soon as I do, cover it with the towel. I'll prepare a bandage when we're done. If you're prepared, blink your eyes twice," Ryan said as he turned and looked down at her face.

She blinked twice and bit the towel.

With his left hand, he pressed down on Dana's hand, holding it tight to the towel on the table. With the scalpel in his right hand he carefully positioned it over her finger and placed slight pressure against her finger with the rear portion of the blade. After taking a slight breath, he paused, and pressed the blade down and pulled the scalpel back, dragging the surgical blade across the flesh of her finger. As the scalpel moved, the blade sliced through her flesh with minimal effort.

Ryan's eyes widened as the blade of the scalpel cut through the fleshy tip of Dana's finger. Although his hands remained steady for the procedure, his stomach began to flutter. With a hint of surprise in his mind, he fought the jittery feeling and pressed the blade through her finger and into the towel.

As Dana bit against the towel she focused on the wall in front of her, and did not watch the scalpel, Ryan, or see the blood. As the blade slid across her finger, it sliced a quarter inch of the tip of her finger off, leaving a square bloody fingertip exposed. Dana continued looked straight ahead, not even realizing that the procedure was complete.

Ryan reached across the table for the alcohol. "See? It wasn't that bad at all."

Dana looked down as her finger began to bleed; now realizing that Ryan had completed his sickening but simple task. With her right hand she covered the tip of her finger with the small towel, stopping the bleeding. Quickly, she uncovered it, looked down at the severed tip, and then covered it again.

"Towel. Please move the towel," Ryan requested quietly.

As Dana complied, Ryan wiped the tip of her finger with alcohol, and covered it with an alcohol soaked bandage. As he did, Dana stared straight blankly at the wall.

Ryan wrapped the soaked bandage with another dry one. "I'm certain that *this* hurts more than actually being cut.

Using the medical tape, he secured the dry bandage to the tip of her finger. When finished, he lifted her hand and admired at his handi-work.

"Well, that looks like it was prepared at a professional establishment, doesn't it?" Ryan asked.

Dana lifted her right hand to her mouth and removed the towel. As she placed the towel on the table, she looked at her left index finger. Uncertain if it was from adrenaline, God's provision of strength, or that there were very little nerve endings in her fingertip, she felt satisfied that there was really no pain associated with what had just happened. As Ryan carried the scalpel to the other side of the table, she closed her eyes and thanked God.

She watched as Ryan sat down, methodically cleaned the scalpel with alcohol, and placed it back onto a clean towel. As he sat down, she wondered if the other women would be given the same options, and if so, the procedure would be the same. As Ryan removed the gloves from his hands, she glanced at his face.

"Well. I have some paperwork for you to sign. We didn't go into detail, but I have some documents for you to sign, stating that you subjected yourself to a psychological experiment from the date you arrived until today. I am a Doctor of Psychology, and you'll sign something stating that you volunteered for an experiment which may include certain deprivations of the mind. It will, of course, be backdated to the day you *disappeared*. Additionally, and as discussed, I will pay you for your time." Ryan reached for the stack of money, and pulled a pile toward where he was seated. "Here is one hundred thousand dollars. Take *that*," Ryan paused and slid the money across the table toward Dana, "Compared to the amount of money I made today, it's nothing. Chump change. Also, it may help you with what you need regarding your cancer."

"You *know* about the cancer?" Dana asked softly as she looked up at Ryan.

"Oh absolutely. I know *everything*." Ryan chuckled. "Now, if you'll stand up and follow me upstairs, we can get you cleaned up and taken back to the city. Wave for the camera."

Ryan pressed the button on the remote control. As he turned the camera off, Dana wondered if he had any additional *off camera* plans. She tried to digest leaving, going home, and being free, but she wondered if this was truly over. As Ryan stood and began walking to the door, she felt a little more at ease.

Standing in the doorway, Ryan turned to face her. "Leave the tip of the finger, Dana. You don't get to take it with you. Come on now, grab your money and follow me."

Puzzled, Dana picked up the stack of money and turned toward the door. As Ryan walked through the door and into the main body of the basement, she felt a little more at ease with the situation. With each step, she began to feel less likely that something else was going to happen. Maybe, she began to think, Ryan *was* a man of his word.

With each step of the stairs, Dana felt a little less apprehensive about following Ryan. His demeanor, his attentive nature, and his personality in general had become light and more human as each second passed. As they walked into the house, Dana was amazed at the cleanliness and organization of the home and its décor.

Clutching the money, Dana followed Ryan as they walked through the home. The home was magnificent, and every available space was covered with a piece of art, a sculpture, or some form of decorative furniture. As she followed Ryan through the home, she admired each form of art she passed.

"In anticipation of your choice of disfigurement, I had your vehicle cleaned and filled with fuel. It did not have a navigation system in it, so I purchased a small Garmin system and temporarily installed it on the dash. It should allow you to get home without much trouble what so ever," Ryan said.

Dana followed him into the kitchen.

"My car is *here*?" Dana asked, puzzled.

Ryan clapped his hands together lightly as he sat down at the kitchen table. "Oh yes, I brought all of your vehicles here as soon as I was able. Now, let us get this paperwork signed and we'll go over the rules of release, shall we?"

Ryan tapped the chair beside him lightly with his hand. "Sit, please."

As Dana sat, she became more comfortable that she was, in fact, going to be home soon. She placed the money on the table and slid it to her left side, away from where Ryan was sitting. As he began to speak, she thought of the women in the basement, what grief they were going through, and what more they would be subject to.

As Ryan spoke, Dana closed her eyes and listened.

And she prayed.

CHAPTER NINE

THOUGHTS OF DYING.

NINE. Elena stood over Meghan, who was seated beside Shellie on the bench.

"So, what the fuck are we gonna do little miss know it all?" Elena asked.

Meghan had spent the majority of the previous night comforting and preparing Dana for her *departure*. Describing it as a departure made it more reasonable, more realistic, and less permanent than calling it anything else. Meghan now dressed in sweats and a tank top like the other women, sat with Shellie, hoping that nothing bad had actually happened to Dana. Although she had no basis for this belief, her considering it made everything Ryan was doing seem plausible.

"I don't fucking know. To tell you the truth, I really didn't think he'd take Dana. I felt like it would never come down to that. I don't know. *I just don't fucking know*," Meghan complained.

Elena sat down on the bench beside Shellie and leaned forward, resting her forearms on her thighs. "Well, if we don't have a plan, this is gonna get really shitty really quick."

Meghan stood from the bench and placed her hands on her hips. "Like it's not *already* shitty."

Shellie rotated her hand and looked at what little was left of her fingernails. "Dana's gone. It's bad already."

Elena stood from the bench and faced Meghan. "This crazy fuck. We have to try to kill him when he comes back. We *have* to. We don't have an option."

"How?" Meghan asked.

"Well, fuck. I don't know. Let's talk about it," Elena said. "When he had me in the basement talking to me, he had a Taser. He didn't have a gun. He had it and handcuffs. He's strong, but he can't overpower three of us."

Elena motioned toward Shellie who continued to nibble at her fingernails as the two women spoke. "Well, two. Two of us. She ain't got much to offer."

Meghan's eyes shifted toward the door. "Ok, so when he opens the door, what do we do?"

"The door pushes *into* the room. There's a handle outside, in the basement, not an inside handle. We can't grab it and pull it. We have to just try to overpower him, or we all rush the door? What are you thinking?" Meghan asked.

"Well, when he opens it, when we hear it click, two of us could be right there, and be ready for his ass. And just take off running. Fuck I don't know," Elena said.

"If we do that, what could go wrong?" Meghan asked.

No one responded.

"I guess, if he pulls it open and sees us - he just pulls it shut and leaves us here forever to die. That's what his crazy ass would do. So, we have to be on the side of the door that he can't see," Meghan reasoned.

Elena appearing frustrated, walked over to the far side of the room and stared at the door. As she crossed her arms and stared, she shook her head. "That doesn't do us any good. Because then we gotta get to the opening, and he'll just see us whenever we try and move over there."

For Elena to allow herself to be taken into the other room, tortured, killed or even released, was going to be a chore for anyone, and Meghan could see and sense it. Elena had become far more tense since Dana had left, and she was outwardly showing it. When the time came for Ryan to come and take Elena from the room, he was certainly going to have his hands full. As Elena started cussing in Spanish and staring at the door, Meghan began to wonder what problems Elena's demeanor could cause if she irritated Ryan.

Meghan believed that she had heard a car leave the garage thirty minutes after Ryan had taken Dana out of the room. That would be roughly the amount of time it would have taken Ryan to kill Dana, prepare the body for transportation, load it, and leave the premises from what Meghan could figure. The other women complained at Meghan's request for confirmation of what she had heard, claiming that they heard nothing.

Meghan pointed to the benches beside her, behind where the door swung when opened. "What if *this*. What if, when he takes Shellie to the door, we're back here."

All eyes were on her.

She walked in the direction that she was pointing. "Where we were before, when he got Dana?"

"We haven't decided if *I* was next," Shellie said softly without looking up from her fingernail gnawing.

"Well, when he comes to the door, he will ask her to turn around. She's slow at everything she does, and she can turn *really* slow, taking a little extra time. He'll become frustrated at her, but not at us. As he waits for her, we rush the door, and yank it open. Whoever gets to the door, the other one will, with Shellie's help, overpower Ryan. How's that sound?" Meghan asked as she faced Elena, who still stood along the far wall.

Elena shook her head. "It sounds like we're trying to plan putting up a volley ball net for a fucking beer party. What if this thing goes to shit? We're fucked. *El Mero Chingon* comes in, and we're just fucked."

"You know. We can do all this planning we want, and this fuckers gonna make it impossible to do it just by one little change in how he opens the door or how he does something. Then, we're sitting here stupid. And dead. Fuck this *puto.* I want to choke him or dig his eyes out when I'm in the other room. When he takes me to kill me, I'm gonna head butt that fucking *pendejo.* Maybe, when he takes me, I'll kick him in his fucking *cajones.* " Elena said.

Meghan, began walking through the room and attempting to devise a plan of escape. She considered seducing Ryan if the opportunity presented itself. She was convinced from the moment she sat in the trunk and made eye contact with him that he was attracted to her. Her discussions with the other women, although she had not outwardly spoken of her thoughts and feelings, had invited the other women to discuss their feelings. She had no information volunteered to lead her to believe that any of the other women had either an opportunity or an indication that Ryan was in the least bit attracted to them.

Meghan stood between the entrance door and where Elena was standing as she thought of Ryan. "Let me just think for a while."

Generally speaking, Meghan believed she was a very good judge of a person, their thoughts, and what they were feeling. Ryan may be psychotic, or he may simply be very calculating, planning, and compulsive. She wasn't able to know for sure. She believed, based on what she knew about people in general, that he was attracted to her. Ultimately, would that mean that she could convince him to act on his feelings? She couldn't decide. She did know if she didn't try, she'd never accomplish it. Exhausted from lack of sleep, she leaned against the wall, closed her eyes, and thought of Ryan and his very handsome appearance when he opened the trunk of the car. As her eyes closed, and she began to relax, she slumped to the floor.

As Ryan opened the trunk lid, Meghan sat up in the large open trunk. Sore from the trip, she shrugged her shoulders and looked up into his steel blue eyes. Ryan looked down and smiled a slow smile. Meghan was surprised by his masculine features and soft boyish skin. His average height was overshadowed by his strong muscular appearance. Even though he wore slacks and a dress shirt, his muscular build was apparent through his shirt as it clung to his pectoral muscles.

Meghan wanted him to remove the tape from her mouth. As he reached into the trunk, she itched for his touch.

"I'm going to remove the tape from your mouth. Do you hear me you cute little bitch?" Ryan asked.

Uncomfortably aroused, she knew nothing more than to nod her head. She was already wet from her thoughts as they had driven, and now – looking at Ryan made it much worse. As she shifted the weight on her hips in the trunk, she felt the depth of her wetness between her legs. Embarrassed, she looked down and then immediately back up at Ryan.

She nodded.

He pulled the tape from her mouth quickly. Eagerly, she began to speak.

"What are you going to do to me?" Meghan cooed.

"My name's Ryan Capshaw, and I'll do whatever I fucking want,

Meghan. You know why?" Ryan asked as he rubbed the palms of his hands up and down the length of his thighs.

"No?" she breathed, wondering how he knew her name.

"Because you're mine. I own your little ass from here on out. I took you from your meaningless life, and now you belong to me," Ryan bragged.

"Sit up straight," he demanded.

She sat up straight in the trunk, pushing her chest toward him as he spoke. He appeared to notice her efforts, and glanced in the direction of her breasts as they heaved forward. As he focused on her chest, she raised her cuffed hands behind her back, straining her shoulders, and forcing her breasts even further toward him.

He leaned forward and peered down at her. "Your boobs are bigger than the other girls."

He was so close that she could feel his breath on her neck as he spoke. She wasn't familiar of the scent that he wore, but she knew from this day forward, she would never forget it. He placed his right hand on her neck and squeezed lightly.

"I'm going to lift you out of this trunk, Meghan. I'm not going to have any trouble from you, am I?" he asked as he squeezed her neck with a little more force.

Her mouth opened, and an almost inaudible 'no' escaped as Ryan leaned forward, his waist now within inches of her face.

She felt his free hand reach to her breast. Naturally, she pulled away from his grasp.

"What the fuck are you doing, Meghan? Don't resist me. Do not ever resist me, do you understand?"

"Yes," she whispered.

He squeezed her breast through her shirt.

Meghan felt herself become even more aroused as Ryan fondled her breasts. He reached down with his right hand and lifted the front of her shirt, exposing her bra. As he tried to lift if further, he became frustrated that her handcuffs prevented the removal of the shirt from her torso. Aggravated, he growled under his breath and removed a knife from the pocket of his slacks.

"Don't move. I don't want to cut you. At least not yet," he said as he used the knife to slice the shirt that he had bunched into his grasp.

As he tossed the shirt in the trunk, he folded the knife and placed it back into his slacks pocket. His right hand now reached back to her throat, squeezing it firmly as he pulled her bra up, exposing her breasts.

He unbuckled his belt and removed his slacks. "Hold still, Meghan."

As his slacks fell to the floor of the garage, he removed his shoes and kicked his slacks a few feet beside where he stood. Now standing before her in stark white boxer briefs, the muscles in his legs flared as he repositioned where he stood. The bulge in his briefs provided reassurance that he was very well endowed.

Sitting upright in the trunk of the car, her shirt cut in two and on the floor of the trunk, Meghan yearned for Ryan to touch her. Five years without a husband, mate, or any form of sexual contact had left Meghan with a burning desire for what she believed that Ryan offered her. As Ryan pressed his briefs with his thumbs, pushing them past his now hard cock, she shifted in the trunk and leaned forward in anticipation.

"Open your mouth," Ryan demanded.

He dropped his briefs in the pile of clothes beside the car. Without hesitation, she closed her eyes and opened her mouth, waiting for his cock to be forced deep into her mouth.

"Open, Meghan. Your eyes will be open," Ryan demanded.

She opened her eyes and mouth at the same time. "Yes, Sir."

Her hands cuffed behind her back and helpless, Meghan leaned forward with an open mouth. Ryan stood before her, naked from the waist down, stroking his cock slowly. As the anticipation mounted, she watched him stroke himself to a full erection. As he leaned toward the edge of the trunk, she moved closer, hoping to feel his cock throbbing in her mouth. His hands reached for her breasts, pushed up by the bra beneath them, and began to squeeze.

As he squeezed her breasts in his strong hands, the tip of his cock was within a fraction of an inch of her lips. He leaned back and began to moan. As his moans became louder and more pronounced she licked her lips and leaned toward his cock, taking the thick shaft into her wet mouth.

"That's a good little bitch. Now suck that cock like you'll be killed if you don't," Ryan demanded.

She pressed her tongue against the bottom of the shaft. With her hands still cuffed behind her back, and slid her mouth up and down the shaft of his swollen cock, feeling the tip against her throat as she tried to force more and more of it into her mouth. Ultimately, she wanted him to be pleased with her performance, and tell her so.

If he chose not to speak, so be it.

As she sucked his cock, he moaned repeatedly as he arched his back, forcing even more of himself into her mouth. Circling the head with her tongue, he growled lightly under his breath as he squeezed her breasts harder. She wanted him to cum - cum in her mouth, all over her tits, or even on her face, she thought. If he would cover her in his cum, there was no doubt he would certainly be pleased with her performance.

She began to moan as she sucked faster and faster, trying desperately to please him. She began to groan as she sucked, the sounds of their moans echoing through the garage. As he moaned, he pulled his hands from her breasts and pulled his hard cock from her mouth. As she looked up into his eyes in disbelief, he forced his cock between her breasts and squeezed them together.

"Meghan, I'm going to fuck your big titties, don't you dare move," Ryan demanded.

As Meghan arched her back, Ryan thrust against her chest, his cock sliding between her fleshy boobs, the tip escaping through the uppermost portion of Meghan's breasts as he forced himself between them.

She watched as his cock slid between her breasts.

As Ryan fucked her chest without reservation, he began to feel his cock swell, and his breathing become labored. He placed his hands on her shoulders and pulled his cock from between her breasts. As he stepped away from the rear of the car, he moved his hands to her armpits and lifted her from the car.

"Ryan, what are you doing?" Meghan asked as he pulled her from the car and held her suspended above the garage floor.

He turned her body to face away from him. "Straighten your legs."

As she straightened her legs, he lowered her to the floor, until her feet touched the concrete. Once her feet were on the solid floor he released his grasp from her armpits, and lifted up on her hands, which were still handcuffed behind her back. As he lifted, to relieve the pain, she bent at her waist.

As her waist bent, he pressed her head into the trunk of the car, and lifted on her cuffed arms.

"Get your head in the trunk, you cute little bitch," Ryan growled.

As Meghan allowed Ryan to pull up on her hands, and force her into the trunk, she felt his hands on the waist of her pants. His hand fumbled for the clasp in the front. As soon as he found the zipper, she felt her pants fall to the floor, and her panties being pulled down past her thighs.

"You're not going to..." Meghan began.

Ryan pressed his hand into the middle of her back, forcing her into the trunk. "Not one word, Meghan, keep your mouth shut. You're mine."

Meghan felt the tip of his rigid cock begin to penetrate her. As she felt the shaft enter her wet pussy, she began to moan. As he forced his length into her, she immediately began to reach orgasm.

"Oh God, I'm," she moaned.

Ryan's hand slid past her chin and covered her mouth firmly.

"Not a word or I'll tape your mouth again," he growled.

He forced himself in and out of her now dripping wet pussy. As she screamed, her voiced echoed through the trunk of the car and into the garage.

Elena shook Meghan's shoulders. "What the fuck, Meghan? Were you having a bad dream? You were screaming."

Confused and feeling sexually aroused, Meghan woke up and looked around the room. She wiped her lip, and realized she had been slobbering as she was dreaming. Embarrassed, she stood and looked at Elena. She gazed at her hand and wiped her mouth again with her forearm.

"I'm exhausted. I was dreaming. Sorry, what did I say?" Meghan asked.

"You didn't *say* anything, you just started screaming. Shellie fell asleep a little bit ago. You were out for quite a while." Elena paused and studied Meghan's face. "You look like shit."

Meghan looked down at her sweats and straightened the waistband. As she tugged the wrinkles from her tank top, she looked back up at Elena with a feeling of guilt settling in her mind.

"Do you think Ryan is attractive?" Meghan asked.

After she spoke, she wished she would have worded her sentence differently.

Elena scrunched her brow. "What the *fuck*?"

"What you mean, *attractive*?" Elena took a step back and crossed her arms as she developed a more disgusted look on her face.

"Yeah, never mind." Still feeling embarrassed, Meghan attempted to dismiss the question.

"No, what you mean?" Elena asked before Meghan had even finished her sentence.

Meghan looked down and focused on her tank top again as she tugged the wrinkles from the fabric. "I just was wondering. I don't know - we kind of talked about it before. It's no big deal."

Elena crossed her arms and narrowed her gaze. "I didn't say it was a *big deal*. It's just fuckin' weird. You wake up and wanna know if I think the sickening prick that's gonna cut us in pieces is a good looking guy. You know, I kinda like you. But you're *weird*. You asked questions about him when you first got here. What the fuck?"

"I'm sorry, I was just dreaming, and I got kind of distracted and confused," Meghan admitted.

Elena uncrossed her arms and tossed her hands up. "What? You were dreaming about *him*?"

"No," Meghan lied. "I was just dreaming, and I was confused. Let's talk about something else."

"Yeah, that's fine. If we're talking about him, I wanna talk about trying to poke out his fuckin' eyes." Elena gestured jokingly toward Meghan's eyes with her finger.

Meghan raised her hand defensively, rubbed her eyes and wondered if her attraction to Ryan was really as odd as it seemed to be. Setting the abductions and killing aside, she felt as if he was an attractive man, had attractive qualities, and behaved in an attractive manner – at least what she had seen of him. She began to wonder if they had met under different circumstances whether she would be attracted to him. After pondering her thoughts for a moment, she was certain she would be.

Meghan stood before Elena knowing that she had entertained fantasies about rape since before she and Mark were together. Through somewhat of a moral inventory, she initially dismissed it to her desire for affection from Mark, and him not acting on that desire. She felt worthless, lacked self-esteem, and began to fantasize even more as the years passed.

This fantasy wasn't something she constantly thought of, or even desired with a degree of frequency. But it lingered. It lingered, and from time-to-time, she masturbated to the thought of being raped. This masturbation led to additional and more frequent mental desire - and the desire led to more repeated masturbation. She learned through interest that developed in her *kink* that four out of ten women have deep seated rape fantasies. After learning of this statistic, she dismissed her feelings as *normal*.

At this particular moment, Meghan felt far from normal.

"What are we going to do?" Meghan asked Elena.

"We can't make a *plan*. It won't fuckin' work. Not in this stupid room. He'll open the door." Elena motioned to the door, clearly frustrated. "He'll see us, and he'll shut the fucker. Probably come back and make us his new stain on the floor."

She turned from Meghan and began to walk the perimeter of the room. "So, if you have any ideas, I'll listen. I think we should just try and jump him when he comes."

Meghan rubbed her eyes, trying to clear her head of the thoughts of Ryan that lingered from her dream. "What time is it."

"I looked a minute ago, it was like seven. You don't want the music on do you?" Elena asked.

"No. I want to think. At night, right? Seven at night?" Meghan responded.

"Yeah. Night," Elena said.

Elena was confident that Shellie would be next. Although Shellie had not actually committed to die next, she was receptive to her family being taken care of should either she or Meghan live through this nightmare. As Elena walked, she began to contemplate the inevitable.

She would not, regardless of circumstances, forfeit her life. Elena had too much pride, too much fight, and too much will to live. If Ryan wanted to kill her, it would be during a fight – a rejection of his will. She filtered her hair through her fingers, and looked at Shellie – still sleeping on the bench.

"How you think this fucker found us?" Elena asked Meghan as she passed by Shellie.

"I don't know, we talked about it. He's obviously got something for brunettes," Meghan said.

"Seriously? That's your fucking answer? He likes brunettes?" Elena scoffed.

Meghan looked up at the ceiling, rested her elbow on her knee, and placed her hand on her chin. Ryan must have an attraction to them, she thought. If he were attracted, why, she wondered, would he find value in killing them one at a time. She began to wonder if it was an attraction or a form of hatred.

"Why don't you think he just killed us all at once?" Meghan asked.

Elena chuckled. "What? That didn't make sense. I'm Mexican, you're from here. Use your words, Meghan."

"How come he didn't just kill us on the street? Or bring us here and kill us? Why didn't he do that? You think he wants to torture us?" Meghan reasoned.

"Maybe. I don't know." Elena stopped and turned to face Meghan. "What you gettin' at?"

Meghan stood from her seat and slipped her feet back into her sandals. "I'm thinking. Why would a guy pick us all up, bring us here, and then pull us out one at a time to kill us?"

"Because he's fucking *crazy*?" Elena answered with a sarcastic tone.

"Didn't you see Silence of the Lambs? And that Spider movie. Along Comes a Spider? People kill just because. They cut off your hands and toss you in the street. Just because. *Because they're weird.* Because their momma didn't breast feed them. Or their dad spanked them too late in life," Elena said, her voice conveying her level of frustration.

Meghan shrugged. "No doubt he's crazy. I just wonder why."

"Why?" Elena asked. "You think if you figure it out - tell him what you think - and you're right, that he'll let you go? He won't. He'll cut your throat for bothering him. He's fuckin' *crazy*."

Meghan shrugged.

Elena sighed. "I'm getting nervous. So, you really got that money? The money you told Dana you had? For taking care of her family?"

Meghan turned toward the bathroom. "Uh huh."

Elena scoffed. "Don't sound too convincing to me."

"I don't know what you *want* me to say. Mark inherited it, we divorced, and I got half. It was a pretty simple procedure. I have never remarried or anything." Meghan finished speaking, turned on the faucet, and rinsed her face in the sink.

As Meghan dried her face, Elena leaned on the doorway of the bathroom. Greed, she began to think, caused and solved many of problems that the world faces today. People are driven by greed to do things they would not normally do.

"So, you think you could buy our way out of this?" Elena asked as Megan hung her towel over the towel bar on the wall.

Meghan wiped her hands on her sweats as she walked toward the doorway. "I don't know, it's *possible*. I suppose it's worth a try. It sure isn't going to do me any good if I'm dead. All of this is just, well, weird. I thought after Dana left...I don't know. It's hard to explain. I thought after Dana left that this would end. Or it'd never get to us. But he's going to come back. He is. Over and over. And we're going to have to kill him or figure out a way to stop him - or change his mind."

"Now you're thinking. We have to kill this fuckin' guy. We do. *You and me.* Because little miss *hueva* over here." Elena motioned toward Shellie. "Isn't gonna last very long."

"Ryan's coming back, and he's got one more to kill before he starts killing *us*," Elena said.

And at that moment, as the two women stared into each other's eyes, the thought of dying – for the first time, began to become real.

CHAPTER TEN

EVER DO ANYTHING SHADY?

TEN. Entering the parking lot, Ryan made note of Ami's car parked in the employee parking area. His heart began to race as he thought of her new hair color, and the tattoo that she had attempted to hide behind her hair. As he parked he turned down the music. Quietly, he closed his eyes, relaxed, and thought of what he may want to discuss with Ami. As he sat and relaxed, he began to think of his father and the advice he received from him as a child.

"You'll never amount to anything but a pile of worthless shit, do you understand me?" his father asked.

"Yes, Sir," the 11 year old Ryan responded.

"Repeat it," his father demanded in a harsh tone.

Standing naked once again, Ryan began to whimper. He wanted to get dressed, go upstairs, and be with his mother. He didn't want to repeat it. When he repeated it, he felt as if he would never be like the other kids. Often, he wondered how long he'd actually live before his father killed him. He was certain his father wanted to, only time and his father's patience preventing it from happening.

"If I have to ask you one more time," his father paused and reached into his pants pocket.

"I am a worthless pile of fat shit. I will always be worthless. I will

never amount to anything," Ryan said as he fought back the tears.

"Again," his father demanded.

Ryan lowered his shoulders and looked at the floor. "I am a worthless pile of fat shit. I will never be...I mean I will never amount to anything. I will always be worthless."

"When you slump, it's apparent just how fat you really are. Again," his father demanded as he circled Ryan.

"I am a worthless pile." Ryan paused and began to cry. He reached up and wiped his eyes.

He bit his bottom lip, stopped crying, and began to speak again. "...of fat shit. I will always be worthless."

Eleven, naked, hungry, tired, and humiliated, Ryan looked at the floor and cried.

"Oh Christ, Ryan. You think if you cry that God can hear you? God doesn't listen to fat kids. God is so fucking ashamed of you. You create problems for God because you even exist on his earth. God is beyond ashamed of your disgusting fat little ass. God fucking hates you. Do you have any fucking idea how I know that?" his father barked.

His bottom lip quivering, Ryan fought back tears as he responded. "No, Sir."

Daily, Ryan wished God would listen. He hoped that God listened to him as he said his prayers at night. He had already lost fifteen pounds, and when he looked into the mirror, the reflection he saw was not overweight.

"Because God talks to me. When I pray, God listens. Do you know why he listens to me?" his father bellowed as he stood at Ryan's side.

Ryan turned and looked at his father. "No, Sir. I don't know why."

The father shook his head and looked at Ryan's naked body with *disgust in his eyes. "Because I am not a fat pile of sickening shit. God hates fat kids, and God hates you. Make no mistake about it. God hates you. If you don't believe me, pray for me to give you mercy. Pray for that. And when God doesn't answer you, when he brings you down to the basement again for a fat inspection, you'll know."*

The father walked around Ryan, studying his body as he did. "I imagine I will not be able to eat that fabulous dinner your mother prepared. Do you know why?"

As Ryan's father circled, Ryan hesitantly responded. "Why father?"

"Holy shit!" his father screamed.

Ryan paused and shook his head in disbelief. "Father?"

"You want to call me father? I do not claim your fat fucking ass. Call me father again, and I will cut you. Sir. That's the word that better fall out of your fat mouth. Sir. Call me father again, I'll take a finger. At least if I did, you'd lose a few ounces. Jesus, Ryan, looking at you is making me sick." His father stood with his hands on his hips and shook his head. "I won't be able to eat that meal, Ryan because I will vomit. As sure as today is Wednesday, and God and I both know it is, I will vomit that roast your mother has so graciously prepared. I will vomit the roast. Now, do you know why I will vomit the roast?"

"No…" Ryan's voice cracked as he tried to speak. "Sir." The tears streamed down Ryan's cheeks as he spoke.

"Because you have upset my stomach, Ryan. You have made me sick. I am sick at my stomach. I will be incapable of swallowing, enjoying, and keeping your mother's wonderful food in my stomach. Because you won't lose weight. One more question. One more, then I must get away from you. Jesus. I may vomit right here. I just may. Ryan, does God love you?" His father stood directly in front of him, and stared at Ryan's bare

crotch.

"No, Sir," Ryan whispered.

"Louder," his father demanded.

Ryan straightened his shoulders and responded. "No, Sir,"

As Ryan spoke, he began to believe his response.

"Because?" his father asked.

Ryan straightened his stance further, looked straight ahead at his father, and responded. "Because I am a fat, worthless, sickening pile of blubber. I am worthless, and I will always be worthless. God hates me, God doesn't listen to my prayers, and he never will."

"You're correct for once in your life. Son of a bitch. Maybe you do know more than how to solve math problems. Well, sleep down here. I am going to try and choke down your mother's dinner. If you're quiet, and I have no reminder that you exist, I may be able to hold it down. Say a little prayer that I am able to eat my dinner," his father said as he turned toward the stairs.

"Oh wait," his father said. "Never fucking mind. Don't say a prayer. I'll just risk it. God doesn't listen to little fat kids. Worthless piles of vile shit. Fat kids that no one will ever want. I don't want to take a chance pissing off God any more than he already is. Just keep your fat mouth shut."

Ryan's father paused and coughed. "I'll do you a favor and tell your mother you're exercising."

His father disappeared up the stairs.

Ryan waited for the footsteps of his father to fade away, picked up his clothes, and got dressed. Now sitting on the edge of the couch and staring at the wall, he began to second guess his self-worth, his purpose on earth, and his faith in God.

Now sitting in the parking lot, Ryan looked at Ami and wondered. As he bit his quivering bottom lip, he rubbed his hands on his slacks and stared through the glass structure into the coffee shop. Filled with admiration for Ami, Ryan struggled with the thought of going inside the establishment and risking rejection.

Ryan turned his left wrist and checked the time. The watch provided a reassurance that he was, in fact, successful. He glanced back into the coffee shop and watched as Ami smiled at the customer she was assisting. Nervously, he looked back down at his watch and checked the time again. After pressing the shirt cuff over the dial of the watch, he opened the door of the car and began to walk inside.

"Good morning, Ryan," Ami said with a smile as Ryan walked through the door.

Ryan raised his arm and looked at the face of his watch. "Good morning, Ami."

"The usual?" Ami asked.

"Yes, thank you," Ryan responded.

He removed a ten-dollar bill and held it in his outstretched arm as Ami pressed the keys on the register. As Ami reached for the bill, Ryan admired the tone and color of her skin. As she took the bill from his hand, he contemplated touching the skin of her hand.

She attempted to hand Ryan the six dollars and various coins. "Here's your change, Ryan."

He searched Ami's neck for a glimpse of the tattoo. "Drop it in your tip jar."

"You're too kind. I hate to even ask but," Ami said. "Well never mind."

"What? Ask, Ami. I have no secrets," he assured her.

"Well," Ami started with a tone of embarrassment. "What exactly do you do? You know, for a living. How do you make your money?"

He crossed his arms and admired Ami's striking appearance. Hesitantly, he responded and waited for her acceptance. "I invest money."

"In what?"

Ryan thought about his investments - his means of making money. He had, as an adult, become obsessed with making money. His successes were a reassurance that he was, in fact, worth something. He was not worthless. He was intelligent, and was a person that was able to plan, prepare, and implement just about any plan to make more money. With his arms crossed across his chest, he turned his wrist and glanced at his watch.

"Well, it depends on what presents itself," he responded.

"Do you ever do anything shady?"

She stopped wiping the countertop and waited for Ryan to respond.

Ryan began to feel uncomfortable. His hands began to sweat. He thought of the women in the room in his basement. He recalled the internet discussions with his Japanese investors regarding the abductions and the game they were going to play – all for financial gain. He began to perform the mathematical calculations in his head regarding one of the women actually choosing death over dismemberment.

He inhaled a breath through his nose, uncrossed his arms, and pushed his hands into his pockets.

Ryan laughed dryly. "Define shady."

Ami looked puzzled. She studied Ryan, smiled, and tilted her head as she reached under the counter and dropped the towel onto the bottom shelf of the cabinet. "Well, some people will do *anything* for money.

You know, they'll do whatever it takes to make a buck. You're young and obviously successful. I just wondered if you got your successes from weird stuff. I was joking really."

She wondered how he succeeded to the degree that he did.

"No," Ryan responded. "I don't. I primarily invest in stocks and some real estate."

Ami reached toward the bar and retrieved Ryan's drink from the barista. As she handed it to him, she smiled. "Interesting, very interesting."

Ryan smiled and reached for the drink. He had hoped to talk about other things, but accepted the conversation as sufficient as he accepted the cup. He raised the cup to his mouth and took a slow sip.

"Taste good?" Ami asked cheerily.

At this instant, Ryan felt as if some things tasted good in his mouth, and some things did not. He lowered the cup as he continued to admire Ami.

"The coffee? Yes, it tastes fabulous," Ryan assured her.

But you must excuse me.

I have women to torture.

For profit.

CHAPTER ELEVEN

WORTHLESS? I THINK NOT.

ELEVEN. With every mile that he drove, Ryan became angrier with his father's treatment of him as a child. His father had constantly reminded him of his weight. Additionally, his father repeatedly explained of Ryan's being worthless. In time, Ryan became to believe his father, and his grades in school were in support of his belief of worthlessness. He had, however, excelled at math - algebra, trigonometry, and calculus. Math, to Ryan, was natural.

Ryan attendance in college as a young adult produced acceptable grades. His earning of a doctorate was never acknowledged by his father. The refusal of the police department to employ him, of course, was acknowledged – repeatedly. He strived to be worthy, physically fit, and successful. His father, however, never recognized him as such.

Ryan pressed the button on the steering wheel with his thumb, turning the volume of the music to a higher level. Music had always been an escape for him, and provided a certain comfort when nothing else could. As the music played, he removed his cup from the holder and took a drink of his coffee.

As he drove, he struggled with thoughts of Ami and what she may believe regarding his investments. It troubled him that she wondered, asked, and had a genuine concern about his means of income.

The women that remained in his home weren't *shady* in Ryan's mind, they were *necessary.* There were no other means that he could use, over any period of time to earn the potential millions he would earn if the women chose the options he had predicted.

His understanding of what the women should choose to do from a psychological standpoint, in his mind, would be accurate. His doctorate, although not applied to his day-to-day activities, allowed him to have a vast and accurate understanding of the women and their respective decisions.

His Japanese counterparts had no such training or opinions.

Ryan believed that he was superior to them in all respects, and the game he was playing would prove his intelligence, understanding of human nature, and his ability to devise and implement such an intricate plan without fault or failure.

CHAPTER TWELVE

FUCK IT, I'LL GO NEXT.

TWELVE. Standing outside the door, Ryan took a deep breath through his nose and exhaled out of his mouth. He looked at the pad on the wall and raised his left hand to the screen. He pressed his left ring finger to the pad, and inhaled another breath. As the magnetic striker released the door, he cautiously pulled it open.

The three women were seated on the bench as far away from the open door as they could be. An unexplainable calm filled the room. The women weren't crying or talking. Quietly, in a huddle, they sat and stared at him as he glared into the room.

"Good morning. Have we made a decision?" Ryan exhaled and waited to continue speaking. "I'll allow sixty seconds for the response."

Ryan turned his wrist and looked at his watch. "Fifty."

Ryan looked up from his watch and into the room. Certain that Shellie was the next victim, He was surprised that the other two girls had not convinced Shellie to be prepared and waiting at the door. Shellie had minimal self-esteem, little income, and a family that she rarely spent time with. She had very little to live for in his opinion – compared to the other women.

Shellie shook her head and stood from the bench. "I'm *not* going to do it."

Frustrated, Ryan stared at the face of his watch as he spoke. "Forty."

"You stupid bitch, if you don't go you're going to die *anyway*," Elena screamed as she stood from the bench and approached Shellie.

"We can all die. I don't care," Shellie shouted as she turned to face Elena.

"Thirty," Ryan barked as he looked up from his watch.

He was becoming more and more frustrated with each second. His financial fate was in the hands of the women, and completion of this task in the order that he had predicted was necessary for him to succeed in the manner he had hoped. His successes would prove his worth as a man of value and intelligence.

"This *loco* fucker is going to kill us." Her voice cracking, Elena's felt as if she had sand in her throat as she spoke.

"Then he can kill us, fine. *You go*," Shellie demanded with a sharp definitive tone.

"*Fuck you*, I'm not going," Elena shrieked as she grabbed Shellie's shoulder and pulled it toward her, turning Shellie around to face her.

Ryan wiped his brow with his right hand. "Fifteen."

"Shellie, we talked about this. *Please*," Meghan pleaded.

"You act like you're asking me to take out the trash or do a chore. I don't want to die. I don't care what the fuck we talked about. *You go*," Shellie bellowed.

"Seven," Ryan shouted.

"Get away from me, you two. *Just get away*," Shellie shouted.

All of the women began screaming at once.

"We'll *all* die if someone doesn't go out there," Elena shouted at Shellie.

Shellie moved to the corner and stood on top of the bench. "*You* go."

"Three!" Ryan screamed.

"Shellie, please. Fuck. *Someone*," Meghan pleaded.

"Two!" Ryan shouted.

"Shellie!" Meghan screamed.

"One!" Ryan looked up from his watch.

"Fuck it. I'll go," a voice echoed from inside the concrete room.

CHAPTER THIRTEEN

UNCLE JOSH

THIRTEEN. Meghan's uncle Josh, in his early thirties, walked into the spare bedroom of his home at 2014 Mountain Road and closed the door behind him.

"If you're going to behave, I will take the gag out of your mouth. Will you behave?" Josh asked softly.

Meghan had been tied to the bed naked for two hours. Scared, tired, and feeling as if she had no other alternative, she stared at the typewriter on the desk and nodded.

Josh knelt beside the bed, reached up over the comforter that was piled beside her and began to untie the bed sheet that was secured tight across her mouth. As he stretched his arm over her chest, his forearm brushed against her nipples.

As her uncle's arm touched her, Meghan flinched. She had stayed at the home of her uncle each summer for two weeks while her parents vacationed. Each time she stayed, he sexually assaulted her for the duration of her time at his home.

Initially, as far as she could recall, the assaults had been oral. It started when she was very young. Initially, she was instructed how to perform on her uncle. Additionally, she was taught how to receive pleasure from him performing on her.

The mental pleasure Meghan received from his initial oral stimulation of her made her feel dirty and guilty. She lived with the guilt each time she reached climax. As hard as she tried to fight the feelings, they continued to come. Based on her fear of disappointing her mother, she felt that she must do as her uncle Josh asked; he was her mother's only brother. Her mother cherished Josh, and Meghan believed denying his requests would certainly be a huge disappointment to both Josh and her mother.

The previous summer her uncle began teaching her how to have sexual intercourse. The entire time spent at his home that summer was filled with sex. Meghan felt tremendous guilt following that summer.

Josh's instructions to her, initially, explained her necessity to perform for him as he requested. Meghan felt that he was, after all, her uncle – and she felt guilty telling him no. He further explained it was an avenue for her to show him how much she loved him and cared for him. Her refusal would indicate a lack of love, Josh assured her. Her lack of love would be explained to her mother, who would be crushed. The sex, without a doubt, would be proof of her love for her mother as well as her uncle.

"God doesn't want us to have hatred in our heart for anyone, Meghan," her uncle Josh had told her that summer.

"If you don't allow me to show you, it means you don't love me. It means you don't trust me. Meghan, it means that you don't care. If you do care, you'll do this for me. I don't want to force you, you must let me. Do you understand?" he had asked.

Meghan agreed *that* summer to allow him to do as he asked. Now thirteen years old, she had a boyfriend. She felt differently about the sexual acts. And she began to feel as if what she had been doing for the

112

last four years was wrong.

"Okay, now have you settled down?" her uncle Josh asked as he stood up, the bed sheet in his hand.

Meghan nodded.

Meghan watched as he removed his shirt and tossed it beside the bed. Meghan felt disgusted by his hairy body. As he rubbed the hair on his chest with his hands, she felt her stomach convulse and heave. She fought back the sickening feeling as he rubbed his hairy body.

"Are you ready?" her uncle asked, his face covered in a hopeful grin.

Desperately, Meghan wanted to shake her head and scream. For the last two hours she had been bound to the bed, her arms and legs tied. Naked, she lay on the bed, shivering and cold. She knew what she must do to please him. Pleasing him was a terrible necessity.

Meghan bit her bottom lip lightly and nodded.

"Say it," her uncle demanded in a soft tone.

"I want you Uncle Josh," Meghan whispered.

"No, say it louder. Like you mean it. Tell me what you want. You know the rules," her uncle pleaded.

"I want you…" Meghan hesitated.

"I want you to…" Meghan's throat felt as if it was full of dirt. Her words barely escaped her mouth.

"I want you to teach me," Meghan muttered.

"That's a good girl. You want me to teach you what, Meghan?" her uncle asked as he unbuckled his belt.

Meghan pulled on the restraints that bound her arms. The restraints were taut, and she knew that there was no relief to speak of. Her pulling against them was a reassurance that she couldn't get away and she was forced to perform as he asked. She relaxed and sighed softly.

"Teach me how to make a man happy," Meghan said softly.

He unbuttoned his pants. "Okay, now all at once. Remember?"

Although Meghan was looking at the foot of the bed, and her uncle stood beside the bed, she could see his pants fall to the floor. As he began to stroke himself to erection, he waited for her pleadings.

Meghan stared beyond the foot of the bed at the typewriter that sat on the desk against the wall. As she focused in the typewriter, she began to speak.

"Uncle Josh, will you teach me how to make a man happy?" Meghan whispered.

He climbed onto the bed. "Yes, Meghan. Yes, I will."

He straddled her neck and began to force himself into her mouth. "Now you know what uncle Josh needs first. Remember? We have to get him wet first. Open up."

With each stroke of her uncle's flesh against her face, Meghan took her mind to a field of flowers in the pasture behind her parent's farm.

They were sunflowers, and often as a little girl, she would run through the flowers and hold her arms outstretched, swiping the stalks as she ran. To her, the flowers were a scented manner of escape. The sweet smell of the flowers filled her lungs, becoming part of her. All of what life included stopped while she was in the field of flowers. While surrounded by the sunflowers, nothing else mattered. Filled with their scent, often she would turn, face the sun, and dream she was a flower as well.

Josh grunted, forcing his weight upon her. As Meghan held her eyes closed tight and ran through the field of flowers with her arms outstretched…

Nothing.
Else.
Mattered.

CHAPTER FOURTEEN

MAKE IT A DOUBLE.

FOURTEEN. "You have to *tell* me how to do this, Dent. Because you sure as fuck aren't going to show me," Ami complained.

Ami had dated Dent for just shy of a year. Their relationship was primarily sexual, which didn't particularly bother Ami. In fact, considering all things, she enjoyed it. Dent left her with an amount of freedom that she was comfortable with, and enjoyed. The sex, generally speaking, was second to none, and Ami expected she'd have a difficult time getting better sex anywhere without a difficult time of trial and error.

Dent pointed to the bed where his friend lay naked. "Jonny, lay flat on your back, and keep your cock stiff."

Jonny relaxed on the bed and stroked his cock, waiting for further instruction. Ami stood beside the bed naked watching Jonny. As he stroked the thick shaft, she began to finger her clit, attempting to keep herself well lubricated. Ami's sexual drive, by her own admission, was extremely high and required a constant level of heightened sexual stimulation to keep her attention and maintain her desire for multiple orgasms.

As she inserted her second finger into her pussy, Dent began to bark out instructions.

"Now you're gonna need to climb up on him and take that in your ass," Dent demanded.

"Dent, I'm tired of your temper, and I will not take that in my ass. I'm down for a double, I am. But you're ruining it for me. One, you need to stop screaming at me. Two, I ain't gonna take Jonny's cock in my ass. It's the size of my wrist and ten inches long. I'll take *yours* in my ass and *his* in my pussy. That's the deal." Ami's voice rose as she spoke.

Dent pointed at Ami's crotch. "I ain't letting him fuck that pussy."

"Okay fine. No deal," she said.

"Okay, fuck it. Fine. Get up Jonny. I'll need to lie down," Dent shouted.

Dent's temper often became elevated for any number of reasons. Although he never hit Ami or caused her a tremendous amount of dissatisfaction, he had slapped her a few times. Slapping, to Ami, was not abuse. She viewed it, right or wrong, as part of *doing business* in a relationship.

As Dent climbed onto the bed, he grabbed the tube of lubricant from on top of the dresser. As he lie on his back, he began to stroke his cock and liberally apply lubricant as he did so. Within a matter of seconds, his cock was hard, and glistened with lube.

"No, get up here, and face me, and lower your ass onto my cock. When I get in that ass, let me get a few strokes. After I'm good and in her ass, Jonny, you get *your* ass up on my lower legs. My calves, whatever, facing me, and just straddle my legs. Just kinda stand there, squat, whatever." Dent waved his hand over his thighs as he spoke. "Then, you bend over, Ami. And lay your head on my chest or shoulder."

As Ami listened she slid her fingers inside her now soaking wet pussy. The thought, to her, of having two cocks inside of her at once was a huge turn on, and not something that she had ever done. She and Dent had talked about this for some time, and now that the time had come, she was beyond ready. As she pressed her fingers up to her knuckles and closed her eyes, Jonny began to speak again.

"And Jonny will…" Dent hesitated. "Fuck, are either of you two shit-heads listening?"

Ami opened her eyes and looked at Dent as he sat up on the bed.

"Yeah," Jonny said as he stroked his massive cock.

Ami closed her eyes and tried to reach climax. "Yep, got it."

"You fuck bubbles. If you were listening, you'd know we got it backwards. Jonny, you got to be lying on *your* back. Same instructions, but you got to be in her pussy. You're on your back. We straight?" Dent bellowed.

"Yep," Jonny said.

Dent slid off the side of the bed.

Ami opened her eyes, clearly frustrated at all of the yelling. "Yeah. Straight."

As Jonny got on the bed, Ami climbed onto the foot of the bed. As he stroked his cock, she climbed onto his thighs and immediately lowered herself onto the tip of his cock.

"Easy," Ami said.

He nodded and worked his hips up and down.

"Let me do it, lie still, okay?" Ami asked.

Jonny nodded.

As Ami lowered herself onto Jonny's massive cock, she immediately reached climax and shuddered from the orgasm. Feeling ecstatic and somewhat embarrassed, she closed her eyes, shook her head slightly, and smiled. Facing Jonny, with Dent standing behind her, she started lowering herself onto Jonny's thick shaft again. As she did, she reached in front of her hip with her hand, and started rubbing her clit.

"You go already?" Jonny asked.

"Yeah a small one," Ami lied.

"You fucker. You never cum that quick with me," Dent complained, still standing behind her.

Ami sighed as she lowered herself onto Jonny's cock. "Well, his cock is the size of a fucking arm. There's a huge difference. He hits spots you don't."

Eventually, she found a rhythm that worked for her and felt comfortable. She bit her bottom lip as she had another orgasm. As she opened her eyes, she raised her left hand to her lip, pressing her index finger to her lips. As Jonny smiled, Dent climbed up onto the bed behind her.

Dent pressed his hand in the middle of her back. "Okay, bend over."

"Easy," Ami complained as she eased herself forward.

Ami leaned forward as Jonny reached up and began to squeeze her breasts. Continuing to work her way up and down the length of Jonny's swollen member, she had another light orgasm. As she placed her hands on his chest, she felt Dent slide his lubricated finger into her ass.

Ami bit her bottom lip. "Oh fuck yes."

Dent slid his finger in and out of Ami's ass as Ami continued to ride Jonny's cock. Feeling more satisfied from sex than she could ever recall feeling, Ami provided herself a mental nod of satisfaction for agreeing to allow Dent and Jonny to do this to *her*. As she began to tingle deep inside, she began to believe she was actually doing this to *them*.

"You ready?" Dent asked.

"Fuck yes. Do it. Do it Dent, fuck my ass," Ami begged.

Dent slid his finger from Ami's ass, and she sighed. With care, he began to push the length of his rather large cock into her ass. As he did, she lowered herself to Jonny's chest and moaned. As her breasts smashed against Jonny's chest she looked into his eyes and forced a smile.

"Fuck me, Jonny," she whispered into his ear.

As Jonny's hips began to work up and down from the bed, Ami groaned and bit her lip. The level of satisfaction she felt from being filled with two cocks at once wasn't double; it seemed to be ten times as heightened. As Dent slid his thick shaft in and out of her ass, Jonny pushed fully into her pussy. Deep inside, she could feel their swollen dicks bumping against one another as they fucked her slowly.

"Oh God, I'm going to explode," Ami growled into Jonny's ear.

"Wait," Dent begged as he increased his speed.

"Oh fuck," Jonny moaned.

"Do it, fucking cum," Ami begged as Jonny continued to press his massive cock deep inside of her pussy.

"Oh God," Jonny moaned.

"Choke me," she whispered into Jonny's ear.

Jonny raised his hands to her neck and began to squeeze.

"Harder. Choke the fuck out of me," Ami begged.

As Jonny's hands wrapped tightly around her neck, she began to moan. She opened and closed her eyes as she felt herself beginning to black out. As she felt Jonny's already massive cock begin to swell, her body began to unleash an orgasm that rang throughout her body from her nipples to her vaginal canal and into her ass.

"Oh fuck, I'm gonna cum in you," Jonny screamed as he squeezed her neck harder.

Jonny began to moan as he exploded inside of her. Feeling as if she was being tickled inside as he came with tremendous force, Ami hit his chest. Almost immediately, she felt Dent cum in her ass as he moaned in pleasure.

"Baby, I'm cumming in that ass," Dent screamed.

As Jonny released her neck, she screamed in pleasure – it seemed the orgasm would end her life.

"Oh my fucking God!" Ami screamed.

The sensation filled her body and ran from her crotch to her boobs and back again, over and over - until it eventually dissipated. Uncertain of the amount of time that passed, she opened her eyes and stared at the wall.

"Nobody move," Ami begged as her body shook in climactic bliss.

As she lowered herself onto Jonny's chest and closed her eyes, she felt as if she was somewhere other than earth. Her entire body shook and she exhaled and relaxed her muscles. All she cared to do was bask in this feeling and last forever.

When she awoke, the room was empty. Although this was unlike Dent, she wasn't surprised. She expected that she may have slept for a considerable amount of time, and maybe the boys had left and gone to the bar.

As she stood, shaky legged and walked to the bathroom, she smiled, thinking of the next time they could fulfill this desire again. She truly felt as if she had used them for her satisfaction, and not vice versa. As she entered the bathroom, she saw a note on the mirror, stuck with soap, and drawn on paper with lipstick. She pulled the note from the mirror and read it.

Fucking slut.

Don't bother.

As she shook her head and tossed the note into her trash can beside the toilet, she thought to herself.

The next man she agreed to be with would be different. A kind of different that made her feel comfortable. A man like no other.

As she sat and started to pee, she cried.

For the last time.

CHAPTER FIFTEEN

DYING TO SURVIVE.

FIFTEEN. Elena stood and screamed at Shellie. "You fucking crazy, dumb, stupid fucking bitch. I ought to…"

"Well, I didn't want to die. I wasn't going out *there*," Shellie pleaded as she stood on the bench and pointed toward the door.

Filled with disappointment and anger, Elena felt as if her blood had begun to boil. She was certain if Shellie had volunteered to die next, she and Meghan could determine a means of escape. Now with Meghan gone, she had no avenue of escape or surviving. Elena knew that *she* would never voluntarily give her life to Ryan, and that he would have to earn her departure from this earth.

Elena took a swipe toward Shellie's leg with her arm. "Get down from there, you dumb cunt."

Shellie kicked toward Elena. "Stop it."

Elena swung her arm toward Shellie's leg once again, catching Shellie's ankle in her hand. Gripping Shellie's leg tightly, she tugged on it sharply, pulling Shellie down onto the bench. Shellie hit the bench with such force that she was momentarily disoriented. Now gripping both legs by the ankle, Elena pulled Shellie to the floor.

As Shellie flopped to the floor, her head landed hard against the concrete, befuddling her even more. As Shellie opened her eyes, she saw Elena bend over her and reach for her neck.

Elena grasped Shellie's neck in her hands. "You stupid fucking bitch, I ought to kill you."

Filled with rage and a fear of dying, Elena knelt over Shellie and placed her hands around Shellie's neck and began to squeeze. Shellie attempted to fight Elena from choking her, but in her confused state, offered minimal resistance. Frantically, Elena squeezed harder and harder as she screamed.

"You stupid fucking bitch. I'm going to kill you and put your fucking body at the door," Elena bellowed as her hands tightened around Shellie's neck.

As Elena choked Shellie, she began to feel relief. She felt as if killing Shellie would provide an assurance of her being able to live through this nightmare. As she continued to squeeze Shellie's neck, Shellie's resistance became lighter and lighter.

Shellie's eyes widened as Elena squeezed the little remaining life from her. As Shellie's heart beat its last beat, Elena's rage heightened. Desperately trying to find answers to a question that had no answer, she continued to squeeze Shellie's neck long after Shellie had drawn her last breath.

When Elena realized that Shellie was dead, she released her neck and stood over the body As she looked down at the lifeless body, Elena spat onto the concrete floor beside her.

"Fucking *puta*. Who's next *now*, bitch?" Elena hissed as she kicked Shellie's dead body.

Filled with rage, Elena bent over and grabbed Shellie's ankles. As she pulled the body toward the doorway, she felt as if her accomplishment would seal her fate to a one-on-one fight with Ryan. Elena was prepared to challenge Ryan and she was certain she would prevail.

Elena believed that Ryan was killing for fun. And she, on the other hand, was killing to survive.

And survive, Elena was certain, was what she was prepared to do – at any cost.

CHAPTER SIXTEEN

WHEN I WAS A CHILD.

SIXTEEN. Frustrated at the fact Meghan was the next volunteer, Ryan grabbed the back of the chair across from Meghan and pulled it from the table. As he began to sit down, he recalculated his anticipated profit based on Meghan being the second woman to undertake his torture. As the frustration mounted, Ryan looked up at the ceiling and drew a slow breath through his nose.

He placed his right hand on the top of the table, gripped the edge tightly, and exhaled as he looked down and across the table into Meghan's eyes.

"First, I have a question." Ryan said. "Up until and including this moment, what is one memory you wish you could remove from your memory bank? Only one."

He looked into Meghan's eyes and waited for her response.

Fearing what may be next, and knowing she had nothing to lose, Meghan spoke of what she had never spoken about to another soul on earth. As she began to speak, she closed her eyes.

"When I was nine, my uncle began molesting me," Meghan paused, her voice cracking as she spoke. Tears began to run down her cheeks. "When I was twelve, he began to have sexual intercourse with me. This continued until I was fifteen and my parents were of the opinion that I could stay on my own."

She wiped her eyes free of tears with her fingertips. "I feel that he took so much from me, yet I feel guilty. I know I shouldn't, but I do. To take advantage of a child, to alter their life…"

Meghan opened her eyes and wiped the tears from her face. "Children are innocent and need to be treated with care, respect, and compassion. If I got to choose, I'd remove that memory."

She closed her eyes and shook her head as she cried. "You know what's really weird? What I remember more than anything is the typewriter that sat at the desk. I used to stare at it to clear my mind."

Ryan studied Meghan and thought of what she said. He remembered the basement stairs, and how he had become to detest walking down stairs. He thought of his childhood, knowing his father played a large part in contributing to who he had become. In the absence of his father's actions, he believed he would be a much different person – he certainly would not be in the position he was currently in.

Ryan began to feel compassion. He shook his head and attempted to remain focused on the matters at hand.

"As you can see, there's a camera on the tripod beside me. A light will illuminate as soon as," Ryan said.

He reached across the table toward the remote control for the camera. As he attempted to grasp the remote, his hand shook uncontrollably. Embarrassed, he quickly pulled his hand from the table and into his lap.

"You don't want to do this do you?" Meghan asked softly as she reached for a towel.

Meghan wiped the tears from her face with the towel and placed it on the table in front of her, resting her hand on the towel. She studied Ryan, finding it interesting that he would wear a white dress shirt, slacks, and a black suit jacket if he intended kill her.

Ryan studied Meghan. "It is not a matter of *desire*, Meghan. It is a matter of *necessity*."

"Explain to me how…" Meghan had not finished her thought or statement before Ryan interrupted her.

"Stop!" Ryan barked. "I am not here to reason with you."

"As you can see, there's a camera." Ryan moved his right hand from his lap and pointed toward the camera.

"You're shaking terribly," Meghan stated.

Quickly, he pulled his hand back into his lap. Shaking was a sign of weakness to Ryan. Embarrassed and frustrated, he took another slow breath as he looked at the ceiling. As he exhaled, he looked down into Meghan's eyes. He felt his eye lid began to quiver. Without thinking, he pressed the index finger of his right hand to his eyelid.

"I am going to offer you *options*," Ryan said softly as he pressed his finger to his eye.

Meghan looked over the table, noticing the handcuffs that he had removed, the scalpel, rubbing alcohol, towels, stacks of money and remote control. She considered why there would be such an amount of money on the table before her. Considering all things, she assumed that he was going to offer her the money in exchange for *something*. What, she didn't know.

Meghan turned toward Ryan, focused on his face, and smiled as she ran her fingers through her hair.

"With each option, should you accept it, there will be other potential options associated with the decision you might make."

Frustrated with her smiling, he paused and glared at Meghan.

Meghan's smiling began to trouble Ryan. He removed his finger from his eye lid. As he did, it began to flutter. Again, he pressed his finger to his eye, this time with more force, and drew a slow breath through his nose. He began to think of his father and the day that he cut the tip of his finger off. He had not lost the necessary amount of weight in the allotted time.

He looked down at his lap at the tip of his left index finger.

"Have you a reason to smile, Meghan?" Ryan asked softly and sharply as he looked up, still pressing his right finger to his eye.

"I find you extremely attractive," Meghan responded.

"Enough. *Stop*!" Ryan demanded.

"I will not be coerced into some form of rudimentary psycho-babble trickery on your part, Meghan. This camera." He pulled his left hand from his lap and motioned toward the camera.

Meghan studied his face. His facial features were strong, and his jaw pronounced. As Ryan's hand waved toward the camera, Meghan glanced at his watch. She felt as if she must lure him into *some* form of conversation. She had, at the last second, volunteered to be the next victim – only because she felt as if she could entice him to listen to her. She felt some odd connection to him, and hoped he felt the same way toward her. Considering the value of the watch, and the probability of his pride of owning it, Meghan opted to bring it up.

"The watch, it's a Patek Philippe," Meghan interrupted, rubbing her wrists as she spoke.

Surprised at Meghan's understanding of what his watch was, Ryan beamed with pride regarding her recognition of his time piece. Incapable of hiding his joy, he extended his arm for Meghan to admire the watch further. Discussion of his watch took his mind from his father and to his successes.

Ryan removed his index finger from his eyelid and placed his right hand on the table. "It certainly is. I am surprised you recognized it as such."

As Meghan admired his watch, she noticed the end of Ryan's left index finger was missing. His finger tip appeared square.

Meghan felt if she could make herself seem human to Ryan, maybe she could reason with him. The watch was certainly something he wore with pride, and she believed if she found a common bond with Ryan, he may become compassionate. With the compassion, in Meghan's opinion, he may become more human.

"It's the type of watch my father sells," Meghan offered.

Immediately, a puzzled look washed over Ryan's face. He began to feel warm and uncomfortable.

He stood from his chair and began to circle the table.

"You father is?"

"My father is Brandon," Meghan stated.

"Brandon Finer?" Ryan asked. "You're Brandon Finer's daughter?"

Ryan knew the owner of the jewelry store quite well. Finer's Jewelry Store. Most people believed the owner's name to be Finer, when in fact he had named the store *Finer's* – which had nothing to do with his last name.

"Well, his name isn't Finer. That's a common misconception. He named the jewelry store Finer's because he didn't believe our last name would look good on the store front," Meghan rotated her head and gazed at Ryan's eyes as she spoke.

Ryan, somewhat puzzled, turned and walked to his chair and sat down. He looked at Meghan for a long moment and opened his mouth to speak. Still at a loss for words, he paused and thought for a moment

133

as he closed his mouth. He had done research on each of his victims, but did not verify maiden names – feeling there was no value in doing so.

As Ryan studied Meghan, she felt that she might have inserted a hint of wonder in Ryan's mind. Although her father was the only dealer in the city that sold Patek Philippe, she certainly didn't *know* that he had purchased the watch from her father; and had only hoped that she could find a common bond with him in her knowledge of jewelry.

He turned and looked at the camera, verifying that he had not turned it on. His mind full of many thoughts, he began to calculate his losses if he allowed the game to stop now. There was no clause for breach of contract, and he had never taken it into account. He would, however, be in breach if he stopped the game short of completion. He placed his chin in his right hand, rested his elbow on the table, and thought.

At worst, he suspected, he would not gather the funds for the profit he obtained from Dana's choice of dismemberment over death. As he rested his hand on his chin he relaxed.

Meghan studied Ryan as he thought. He had been silent for a moment or two, and the silence could be either a gift or a curse, depending on what he may be thinking. After another moment of not a word spoken, she opted to again break the silence.

"Ryan, I'm *human*. I'm *real*, and I am the daughter of someone you know. Please, have some compassion and release me and the other two women. What you have already done can't be changed. What you choose to do from here on out can be," Meghan said.

Although Ryan was looking at Meghan, his eyes did not appear to be focused. He seemed to be staring through her, not at her. His mind filled countless thoughts; he began to feel as if he could hear himself think. He shook his head sharply and turned to look at her.

"I need a moment to think," Ryan said sharply. He paused and focused on Meghan for a moment. "The human mind, Meghan. It's an odd tool. We process information and proceed with life having our own belief of *how* to proceed based on our *understanding* of what we have been exposed to in the past. We are a product of our exposures, experiences, and our mind's capacity to process it's understanding of the same."

He rubbed his hands together. "A game Meghan. This, to me, was a game - a game of tremendous planning, deceit, coercion, and a little cunning nature. The same people, exposed to the same trauma, the same events – they all process it differently."

"I do not now, nor have I had any intent of killing. I wanted you to *believe* I had the intent of killing. There's no value of me going into detail regarding the extent of my planning, but let's just say it was an experiment," he said.

"Dana. What happened to Dana?" Meghan asked.

He pressed his hands to the table, moved his chair slightly and stood. He paced back and forth on the side of the table opposite of Meghan and took several slow breaths.

Ryan's fascination with the human mind and its capacity to deal with death had prompted him to consider this experiment over any other. His obsession with money, lack of self-esteem, and self-worth had brought the experiment to fruition – for the financial gain. In his eyes, it was a manner to kill two proverbial birds with one cast stone.

"Most people, short of the insane few that occupy space on this earth, are incapable of killing unless they are doing so to survive. The instinct to survive is quite strong. Statistics support that man will kill to protect the one's that he loves – family for instance. Additionally,

135

some kill as a means of revenge and seem to form an odd justification for having done so. That percentage is, however, small," Ryan said. "I can assure you I am not insane, nor do I have any axe to grind regarding revenge. This experiment, to me, was a means of proving a few things; my understanding of the human mind and its ability to process and deal with death."

He stared blankly.

As he gazed at Meghan's face, he thought of Ami. He had carefully chosen the women because of their resemblance to Ami – and he now realized that Meghan had the greatest resemblance of all of the women.

"I have always been fascinated with death. The absolute end - we *all* fear it. What does the mind go through in the process of planning to survive? What do we consider? Contemplate? It would be one thing to assume or to guess what might happen. But to have *accurate* data, from people that were on the verge of death? That, Meghan, would be priceless in my opinion. Priceless."

He rocked back and forth on the balls of his feet. "I released Dana. You and I have not spoken in detail concerning all of what is sitting on this table, or what my intentions were. But I will offer you this; I intend to compensate you for your trouble. I'm considering some things."

"You fascinate me, I find you interesting," Meghan said softly, trying to lure Ryan into having enough interest in her to consider releasing her.

Sensing Meghan's interest as genuine, Ryan began to boast. "I have a Doctorate in Psychology. I do not practice, however. I am rather secure, financially speaking. I find the mind an interesting place to play. It troubles me."

"What you spoke of earlier, it troubles me. I have attempted to shake it, but it continues to bring me to an uncomfortable place," he admitted.

Meghan looked up at Ryan as he stood before her. She picked up a towel from the table and blotted her cheeks directly below her eyes. She was shocked that she had told Ryan, but at the time, she felt as if she had nothing to lose. Now, she wasn't quite sure where Ryan was going to go with what he originally had planned. He seemed, to Meghan, to be side tracked. She found some comfort in the fact that he seemed to be thinking about her past and not focused on the matter at hand.

"It troubles me too. You're the first person I have told," Meghan admitted.

"The odds…well, the *data* to support my statement, if I remember correctly." He paused and motioned toward her. "There's roughly a ninety-five percent recidivism rate - the rate of recurrence in such acts. I find it troubling."

He pushed his hands into the pockets of his slacks and began to rock back and forth on the heels of his shoes. "Statistical data would be supportive of the fact that he has not nor will he ever stop. For curiosities sake, Meghan, is he a local man?"

He turned and faced Meghan.

Meghan attempted to swallow and looked down at the table. "Yes."

Ryan nodded.

Megan began to cry as she thought of her uncle continuing to do to others as he had done to her. He was not married, and his lifestyle certainly would support him doing so at his leisure. She reached for the towel and held it to her eyes.

He walked back to his seat and sat down. "One last question and we'll move on."

"His name," Ryan said.

Without looking up, Meghan responded. "Josh. Josh Volvo, like the car."

"Very well," Ryan sighed.

Ryan drew a slow breath in his mouth and looked at the camera. "The more I think about that, well...my apologies, I said we were done, let us be done."

The money, at this point, didn't matter. Ryan's focus had changed. Ryan's sexual interest, although he had never physically been with a woman, had started on a BDSM website - Fetlife. Discussing procedures, kinks, thoughts and feelings associated with them interested Ryan. The on-line thoughts had led to some off-line conversations. Eventually, discussions of snuff films began. Ryan had no interest in killing for money, but his psychological background caused him to have tremendous interest in what the human mind may consider when facing death.

The financial gains from the game, when presented to the Japanese business men, were so great Ryan felt this was something he *had* to do. It was not a choice that he spent much time considering. In retrospect, Ryan began to feel compassionate toward the women. As he sat and thought, he attributed it to Meghan and their discussions.

Ryan turned from the camera and faced Meghan. "What are your thoughts regarding me?"

Meghan, still looking down at the table with the towel on her face, looked up at Ryan.

"In general?" she asked.

"In general, yes," Ryan responded.

Meghan thought for a brief moment, intending on answering truthfully. She considered what she *should* say, and contemplated what she *wanted* to say. Her thoughts toward Ryan, she was certain, weren't *totally* natural or normal. She started to speak, paused and started again.

"May I ask a few questions?" Meghan asked.

Ryan crossed his arms and sat back in his chair. "Certainly."

Meghan leaned forward, resting her forearms on the edge of the table. "When you opened the trunk, when we got here - I felt an odd attraction toward you. The majority of the time I was in the room, I thought of you. And to be quite honest, my volunteering to come out of the room? I suspected I could talk you out of harming us. I don't know, I feel attracted to you. I know that sounds insane, but it's true."

Meghan though of her daughter for a brief moment, and realized through the majority of her capture, she had not thought of her daughter consciously. She had no doubts that her daughter was the most important thing in her life - but throughout this period of captivity, she rarely thought of her. She watched Ryan as he repositioned himself in his seat, wondering if mentally separating her daughter from these events was natural.

Feeling somewhat uneasy regarding Meghan's expressed attraction toward him, Ryan began to rearrange his seating position, and crossed his legs. He placed his hands together in his lap and leaned forward.

"That's an interesting thought. Let me think. Had I kept you for six months, and mistreated the others, it would not be too odd for one to assume you may develop Stockholm syndrome. It is something that would present itself in about one in say," Ryan said.

"I'd say one in about ten. But the conditions of your situation here." He raised his hands from his lap and waved them in front of him. "Don't quite support that condition. I find it very interesting. What, if anything, Meghan, do you attribute that to?"

He placed his hands back onto his lap and leaned back in his chair.

Meghan shrugged. "I don't know that I know. It seems really strange sitting here talking to you about it. Actually, I am kind of embarrassed now."

"No, let us continue." The words escaped Ryan's lips before he realized he had spoken.

He was eager to continue the conversation, but he did not want it to appear that he was losing control of the situation. He leaned back into his chair and waited.

Meghan hesitated.

Anxious and eager to continue, Ryan broke the silence. "Meghan I am going to confide things in you. Things similar to what you shared. Things my precious mother doesn't even know."

Meghan nodded, now feeling like Ryan was loosening his grasp of the hold that he had on her. Anxiously, she now waited for him to continue.

"My father, the torturous soul that he is, used to take me into the basement. He would do so about twice a month, from the time I was nine until I was about fourteen. He would make me strip naked, and he would circle me and inspect me. The things he would say."

Ryan stared blankly at the door behind Meghan. "He would circle me and tell me that I was fat and worthless. He said I would never amount to anything because I was a worthless stupid slob. His critical and inconsiderate nature caused me to become healthy and conscious of my weight, but who's to say that wouldn't have happened anyway."

He raised his left hand and extended his index finger. The tip was somewhat square – not rounded like the others. "He removed *that* with a pocket knife in the basement one day – to provide me with a constant daily reminder to lose weight. He advised me he would remove it an ounce at a time if he had to."

"I don't know where I was going with that. It still troubles me about your unfortunate circumstances as a child. But, that matter is off limits for the time being. Well, let's see." He paused and looked into his lap.

Ryan pondered the Japanese business men and their potential reactions to his decisions. He considered what he had done to Dana, and the scheme he had devised - the idea of signing paperwork stating that the women had subjected themselves to psychological evaluations and testing – in his opinion eliminating his risk of prosecution. The longer he thought about it, the more he convinced himself that his plan was not that great of a plan after all.

"Meghan, I believe that we all make a decision in our life that we believe at the time is warranted. Later, when reconsidering that decision, and being honest, we may realize that the decision wasn't warranted after all. This was such a decision."

"Let's release the women from the room, shall we?"

Meghan swallowed, not knowing whether or not to believe Ryan.

"Well, come on now, this was *your* idea. I can't wait to see the expressions on their faces," Ryan said as he walked around the corner of the table.

Reluctantly, Meghan stood from her chair and turned to face Ryan.

He motioned to the pile of money on the table. "I know this isn't much, but I am truly sorry. I will make an honest effort to make it up to you."

Lightly, Meghan shook her head. "Actually, I'm quite well off myself. I have more than I can ever spend."

Ryan laughed as he walked through the door and into the main room of the basement. "You don't say?"

Meghan followed him as he walked to the door of the room Elena and Shellie were in. As he held his hand up to the pad, the magnetic door lock mechanism clicked. Ryan pressed against the door with his palm of his right hand.

The door moved slightly. Ryan pressed against the face of the door again, harder.

The door moved another inch or so. Ryan turned and looked at Meghan as if she held the answer.

"There appears to be something blocking the door," Ryan said with a note of question in his statement.

He placed both hands on the door and pressed against it, leaning with his upper body against the door. As the door opener further, Ryan could see Shellie's hair on the floor. He looked up and toward the bench along the far wall. Elena sat on the bench, holding her knees against her chest with her forearms.

She rocked back and forth on the bench, mumbling softly.

"Oh my God," Meghan gasped.

Ryan looked down at the floor and peered around the edge of the door. Shellie's body blocked the back side of the door. Ryan's precursory view of Shellie's face confirmed what he suspected.

Shellie was dead.

This was not part of the plan.

CHAPTER SEVENTEEN

SURVIVING DEATH.

SEVENTEEN. The magnetic lock clicked sharply as Ryan pulled the door closed. He glanced at Meghan and attempted to maintain a level of composure. He had never imagined the game would have an option of the women being willing to actually kill each other to survive. His suspicions regarding the mind's natural compulsion to survive was stronger than he anticipated. He pressed his sweaty palms to the thighs of his slacks and drew a slow breath.

"I need a moment," Ryan said.

Meghan stared, attempting to process that Shellie was in fact dead. She felt, more than anything, sorrow for Ryan. She was sorry that he thought for even a fleeting moment that this *game* could have anything but negative results. She felt compassion for him having received the torture he received as a child. She thought of Shellie's body, and what would be required next.

She began to wonder what Ryan may be contemplating, considering there was now a body to deal with. Her mind began to race with thoughts of death, killing, and struggling with morality. Ultimately, she didn't want Ryan to feel that killing her was any form of a necessity to prevent her from discussing Shellie's death.

"I saw *nothing*," Meghan blurted softly.

Ryan raised his hand, holding it steadily between him and Meghan. "Stop, please."

"I need to think. Come with." Ryan began to walk back toward the room where they had been a few moments before.

Meghan quietly followed a few steps behind as Ryan walked toward the room. She admired Ryan's walk, which was methodical and precise. Standing perfectly erect, his posture was rigid and formal. Dressed in his slacks, dress shoes, and jacket, he looked like a business man, not a killer.

Ryan sat in his chair and placed his elbows on the table. As he lowered his face into the palms of his hands, he pressed his eyes with his fingertips. As his fingertips massaged his eyebrows, he began to speak.

Meghan quietly sat in the chair on the other side of the table and listened.

"This is nothing short of a God forsaken mess, Meghan. There's not much that money can't fix, but money can't make this repair. I'm having a difficult time determining what my best option is." His voice was muffled by his hands.

Meghan wanted to speak, but waited for Ryan to continue. She could hear Ryan's deep labored breathing through his fingertips. After a few moments, he looked up from the palms of his hands. His eyes appeared to be filled with intent.

A deep desire.

Ryan studied Meghan's face, raised his eyebrows, and drew a slow shallow breath.

Meghan began to feel nervous.

"Listen, Meghan. Things have changed. I cannot risk exposure. That is not an option. This is no longer a game of chance, odds, or collecting data. This has become *real*. I'm quite certain, to you, it has always been real. I, on the other hand, have been on the outside looking in. I have been in control, pulling the strings, calling the shots, making the rules so to speak. *Until now*." He paused and looked down at the top of the table as he lowered his chin into his hands. "I am of the opinion there are no options. Correction; let me rephrase that. I am of the opinion there is *one* option. There are no *choices*."

He pulled his hands from his face, lowered them into his lap, and sat up in his chair. Feeling as if he had solved a lifelong problem, he became filled with the warmth of satisfaction and a glimmer of hope. He was certain that he had determined the only option that could be considered. There was no other option, only the last stage of acceptance. Implementation, in his mind, would present options.

"Meghan, we must kill Elena," Ryan breathed.

Meghan sat up in her chair and stared. She blinked her eyes shook her head in disbelief.

"What? Kill? We? We? *We* must?" Meghan stammered.

"Yes, Meghan, *we*," Ryan confirmed.

He stood from his chair and shoved his hands deep into his pockets. "There is no other way. I have become fond of you. We have a common bond, our childhood. Elena, on the other hand, despises me. I cannot risk her speaking of this. The only loose thread is Dana, and I am struggling with what to do in that regard."

Meghan began to attempt to mentally digest what Ryan was presenting to her. Killing Elena was not something she wanted to be involved with, but she felt as if she couldn't reason with Ryan. She felt that this was something that could still go very, very wrong if she attempted to oppose Ryan's thoughts or processes.

145

"The problem – or problems – in my opinion are as follows…" He pulled his hands from his pockets and rubbed the sides of his head. "If I allow Elena to leave the premises, I or *we* must dispose of Shellie's body. We would become accomplices to murder - as guilty as the murderer. If Elena ever gets caught or decides to say one word, everyone exposed to this is guilty. We would be relying on Elena's ability to live with the guilt, remorse, and mental torture of what she's done."

"On the other hand, if we eliminate her, that would leave you Meghan, you and I. The only two *in the know*, as they say. That now, Meghan, brings me to this." He turned to face her. "You will be the one to kill her. It's the only way."

Meghan began to consider killing Elena, and what Ryan had said. Elena could, in fact, eventually be overcome with guilt, and she may tell the authorities what had happened. She may confide in a family member or a friend. If she were allowed to live through this, she would hold the fate of both she and Ryan in her hands.

The risk of prison began to fill Meghan's mind. Not seeing her daughter, not being an active mother in her daughter's life. Who would raise her daughter? Certainly not her ex-husband – he was not an active participant now, and she was sure that would not change. Prison, Meghan decided, was not an option she was willing to risk. Killing Elena, considering all things, was truly the only reasonable option. Leaving Elena with the knowledge of Shellie's death, knowledge of Ryan, Ryan's name, Ryan's whereabouts, everything - was a great risk.

Without a doubt, Meghan concluded, the risk was far too great.

Ryan was correct, Meghan decided. She would have to kill Elena.

CHAPTER EIGHTEEN

WITH THIS GUN, I DO THEE WED.

EIGHTEEN. Ryan opened the safe. "Are you certain?"

Meghan shrugged. "There's not really another option. Not one that I see."

As she considered what she was going to have to do, the thoughts came surprisingly easy to her. She was surprised that at least for now she was accepting killing another human being. Contrary to how she felt that she *should* feel, it wasn't surreal, or like a bad dream. It was what she believed that she had to do to survive. Killing Elena was not an option, it was a necessity.

And survive was what she was determined to do.

"What about the body? What about the body - or I guess the bodies, after this is over? I don't have to do anything about that, do I?" She asked.

Meghan began to think of the personal nature of disposing of the bodies and actually seeing, touching, and handling the corpses of the women that she was sharing a living space with only hours before.

"I haven't given it much thought," he responded over his left shoulder.

He stood from the safe, a gun in his right hand.

"And you're familiar with the processes? How to handle it? You're certain?" he asked.

"Yes, I have a Conceal Carry Permit. I had to take the silly class. My father made me do it," Meghan responded.

"Well, this is an older pistol," Ryan stated as he held the pistol at arm's length. "Rather collectable, I guess. I purchased it as an investment."

"Colt 45 caliber. Yes, I'm familiar with it. My dad is a gun nut. I'll be fine. Is it loaded?" Meghan asked.

Ryan pulled the upper slide of the Colt back and looked into the breach of the weapon. After confirming there was a round in the barrel of the weapon, he looked up at Meghan and nodded his head.

He held the pistol delicately at his side. "Let's go back downstairs and see if we can devise a plan that is fool proof."

Ryan had purchased the Colt 1911 .45 caliber pistol as an investment. It was in perfect condition, and was of WWII era. A collector had advised him that it was worth $10,000 in the condition it was in at the time of purchase. Ryan's knowledge of firearms was nil, and although he had threatened the women with death, he would have been extremely uncomfortable attempting the act with a firearm. Additionally, his attraction to the firearm was the lack of requirement of necessity to register it. Having the weapon not registered to him was a huge benefit, in his opinion.

He began walking toward the stairs, and Meghan followed a few steps behind him. As they walked, she wondered where Elena would be standing when Ryan opened the door. Elena could possibly try to escape, she thought. Possibly, if Elena was no longer sitting on the bench, she might attempt to overpower them, requiring Meghan to shoot her at close range. Shooting Elena at arm's length wasn't something that appealed to Meghan at all. The thought of it sickened her.

As Ryan walked down the steps, he thought of his father. Since becoming an adult, walking down steps, in general, had become something Ryan always tried to avoid. Additionally, basements, in Ryan's opinion, were evil. With each step he held his breath and clenched the pistol tight in his hand. As he stepped from the last stair, he sighed.

"Do you think she'll look at me?" Meghan asked.

Ryan walked through the door and around the table. "I have no idea. I don't think you should think about things like that to be quite honest,"

He sat at the table and placed the gun in front of him. He considered giving Meghan the gun, and for a moment wondered if she may try to kill him and release Elena. He looked down at the pistol and thought of dying, of killing, and of what he had done to bring these events to the forefront of his life. Considering all things, he regretted beginning this game. As Ryan looked up at Meghan, he decided he trusted her.

Whatever shall happen is truly out of his hands, Ryan thought. If he provided her the pistol and she had opportunity and an option to kill him, but did not, she must truly feel differently about him. He picked the pistol up and reached across the table.

He held the pistol over the center of the table. "Here, get comfortable with it."

Meghan reached for the pistol and looked into Ryan's eyes. He blinked his eyes and exhaled as he held the pistol delicately over the table and waited. As she gripped the barrel and took the weight off the pistol from his hands, he smiled a soft smile.

Meghan looked down at the barrel of the pistol and pressed the magazine release, removing the magazine of cartridges from the pistol. After verifying that it was fully loaded with ammunition, she pressed the magazine back into the bottom of the grip frame and locked it into place. Carefully, she slid the slide of the pistol back and confirmed that a round was in the chamber. After releasing the slide and allowing it to close completely, she cocked the hammer and pressed the safety into place.

As Meghan carefully placed the cocked and loaded pistol onto the table, she looked up at Ryan. A slow nod of acceptance from Ryan confirmed her thoughts of his belief of her trustworthiness. She smiled in return.

Meghan placed her hands in her lap and sat forward in the chair. "What? Did you think I was going to shoot you instead?"

"Had I believed for one moment that you were capable of harming me," he said. "I would not have given you this option. I merely would have retrieved the pistol, shot you, and shot Elena."

Meghan pressed her palms onto the edge of the table and pushed her chair back onto the rear legs as she straightened her forearms. As she balanced on the rear legs of the chair, she smiled. She admired Ryan's dress, and his handsome looks. She smiled and attempted to determine just how she felt about all of what was being requested of her.

She was relaxed. As she realized her degree of comfort, she began to become worried. "I don't know if I really realize that this is actually going to happen."

Ryan tapped his index finger against his lip. "It *must* happen. I suspect we should get down to the details. I will, of course, open the door. As soon as the door opens, be prepared. The first opportunity you have Meghan, shoot. And Meghan, shoot to kill her. I am not interested in watching you shoot her countless times. Or to listen to it. I suspect that the noise will be unnerving in that concrete room. It's a good thing I live in a rural area. Oh, and the entire room is concrete, so don't miss her and hit a wall for goodness sake. We'll have a ricochet that could cause damage to us all."

He cocked an eyebrow and waited.

She dropped her chair onto all four legs. "Don't worry, I won't miss."

Ryan grinned.

Leaning into the table, she laid her forearms onto the top and clasped her hands together. "What happens when this is over? After I shoot her? What happens then?"

"Well. Let us see. We'll get rid of the..." Ryan was in mid-sentence when Meghan interrupted him.

"We?" The thought of handling the dead bodies sickened Meghan.

For now, at least, she considered shooting Elena as something that she had to do. Surviving. If she wanted to get home to see her daughter, to find her daughter, to begin living life again, she must kill Elena. Handling the body, in her opinion, was something she was not prepared to do.

Ryan nodded. "Yes, I will need assistance with the bodies."

Meghan pushed herself from the table and looked down at the pistol. "Get someone else to help you."

"Pardon me?"

Meghan shrugged. "That's the difference between agreeing to do this being involved. I will not mess with the bodies. I can't and you can't expect me to. It becomes too personal. I was in that room with those women. I was reasoning with them, planning, plotting to try to..."

"Yes, I suspect you were," Ryan admitted.

"Well, fair enough. First things first, I suppose. Do you suspect you're ready?" Ryan asked.

Meghan nodded and stood from the table. As she reached down and picked up the pistol, Ryan watched intently. Meghan blinked her eyes, and looked at the pistol curiously. Although she considered it, and felt she should, she didn't say a prayer. She turned toward the door and walked out into the basement and to the doorway, not looking to see if Ryan followed.

Ryan stood from his chair and walked toward the door of the room. As he reached the door, he inhaled a slow breath and stepped through the threshold. As he noticed Meghan standing at the door of the secured room, he exhaled. He stepped to the doorway, raised his right finger to his lips, and adjusted his jacket with his left hand. Feeling an odd level of comfort toward Meghan, he nodded and raised his eyebrows on question.

Meghan nodded in reassurance and released the safety of the pistol. As she stepped away from the door, straightened her forearm, and took a defensive stance with the pistol, Ryan raised his left hand to the pad beside the door.

As the door lock mechanism clicked, Ryan inhaled a slow breath.

Meghan stared at the door and waited as Ryan's began to press against it with both hands. As the door swung open she looked down the barrel of the pistol and held her breath.

CHAPTER NINETEEN

AN ANGEL COMES.

NINETEEN. Elena held her knees close to her chest and rocked back and forth on the bench, her fingers intertwined as her hands continued to shake. After Ryan had opened the door earlier, moving Shellie's body, she could not stop staring at Shellie's face.

Covering Shellie's face with a towel had helped, but it did not relieve the guilt that Elena felt from taking the life of another living being. Filled with disbelief that she had reached a point in a moment of anger that allowed her to justify doing what she had done, Elena rocked back and forth on the bench and mumbled.

Twenty four hours prior, Elena was as far separated from God as she would have ever guessed possible. Now, on the bench, her mind was a flurry of emotion, thoughts, and feelings. Her focus had become God, and as she rocked back and forth, she continued to pray.

Elena prayed for forgiveness, she prayed for strength, she prayed for understanding, and she prayed for her daughter to live a healthy trouble free life. As she prayed for God to forgive her for what she had done, she heard a sharp metallic click.

Methodically, and without care, Elena continued to face the bathroom wall, rocking and praying. Out of the corner of her right eye, she saw the door move. Slowly, it opened. As it did, she prayed to God to give her the strength to die in a manner that was acceptable to him. She begged for forgiveness, recalling that if asked, God would provide.

Elena's elbows on her knees, and her knees on her chest, she rocked and prayed as she waited for her fate to become reality. Whatever Ryan would impose onto her, she would be able and willing to accept. Her mind had become deserving of the punishment that lay before her.

At the same instant of the room being filled with the deafening sound of the pistol being fired, the bullet struck Elena's right side, below her armpit. The impact thrust her left side into the wall, and her body rotated to the right as she instinctively attempted to stand. Her legs incapable of supporting her weight, she faltered and looked up, uncertain of what happened.

As her lungs began to fill with blood, she blinked her eyes. The silhouette in the door appeared to be Meghan.

Coming to save her from this hell on earth.

An angel.

Her angel. Delivered from God to take her to the final resting place. Meghan.

Elena closed her eyes as she waited for Meghan to lift her from the bench. One last apology to God was being mouthed silently as the second bullet entered her chest. The .45 caliber slug tore through her other lung and ripped through the muscles of her back before its travel was stopped by the concrete wall behind her.

As the smell of copper and cordite filled the room, Elena's body slumped onto the bench. Blood dripped from her upper body, over the bench and onto the floor, pooling toward the center of the room. As the mass of ruby red fluid began to gather directly over the stain underneath the epoxy coating, the door closed. And Elena's heart beat one last time.

CHAPTER TWENTY

CAN PIGS FLY?

TWENTY. "Momma, pigs can't fly, ever. Can they?" Amanda asked as she attempted to scoop the remaining few Cheerios from her bowl of cereal.

Meghan laughed. "No sweetie, not ever. Why do you ask such a silly question?"

Amanda reached into her bowl with her hand and pinched the Cheerio with her fingers. "When you were sick, Gram said that. *When pigs fly*. But pigs can't fly."

"Honey, use your spoon." Meghan chuckled as she watched the milk drip down Amanda's arm.

"They keep running from me, Momma," Amanda responded as she poked a Cheerio into her mouth.

The three weeks that had passed since Ryan's release of Meghan had gone by quite quickly. Two more days of school, and Meghan would have an entire summer of uninterrupted time to spend with her daughter. As she watched her daughter reach back into the bowl again, she held her complaint in reserve.

The police had questioned Meghan regarding her memory and recollection of the events. Her explanation of being bound, gagged, blindfolded, and placed into a room was welcomed with watchful eyes and wanting ears by the officers. She further explained that four days later she was blindfolded and released into the city at night. This was noted and unquestioned by the officers.

To date, the bodies of Elena and Shellie had not been recovered.

Meghan felt as if she emerged from the events of her capture a different person. She felt that she was much more understanding, willing to listen, and more capable of believing that as odd as it may seem, everything on this earth happens for a reason. She continued to tell herself the events that happened over the course of those four days were nothing more than a dream. The memories were tucked away with the memories of her childhood, in a place that was safe from the daily recollection that would cause them to haunt her.

Spending time with her daughter, as comforting as it was - caused Meghan to question her inner psyche - her mind's subconscious thoughts. The fact that Meghan had not spent much time thinking of her daughter while she was in captivity bothered her. She struggled with acceptance of her actions while she was in captivity, trying to discern if her thoughts and actions were a defense mechanism, some form of survival skill, or simply denying if it was all real.

As Meghan spooned her last bite of yogurt into her mouth from the cup, she once again wished Ryan was available to talk to her. She had so many questions she wanted to ask, but was incapable of doing so. There was no doubt in Meghan's mind that she loved her daughter, and for now that would have to suffice.

As the spoon circled the empty yogurt cup, Meghan's mind wandered to thoughts of survival. The simple thoughts that she had struggled with, and the ones that came without even thinking at all. Life's difficult decisions becoming simple and without thought. Survival, Meghan decided, was something that the human mind did *without* thinking. As she stopped thinking and watched the spoon circle the cup, she realized that it was long since empty.

Meghan looked up and focused on her daughter.

"Sweetie, are you finished?"

Amanda nodded, unaware of the thoughts that filled her mother's mind. Her hands covered in milk, and her bowl free of Cheerios, her morning was complete and she was ready for what the day might bring.

"Momma?"

"Yes, sweetie," Meghan responded, realizing she was still staring into the empty cup of yogurt.

"Gram said things die because their time on earth is over with, that's what she said," Amanda stated without emotion as she fished her fingers through the bowl of milk.

Surprised at Amanda's recollection and recital of the statement, Meghan lowered her empty yogurt cup and focused on her daughter for a moment. She began to feel uncomfortable, and tried to decide if it was Amanda's statement regarding death, death in general, or thoughts of Elena that caused the uneasy feelings that began to fill her.

"Baby, what was she talking about when she said that?" Meghan asked.

Amanda slid out of her chair and onto the floor. "Chancey died, momma. He wasn't at Gram's when you were sick. He was gone. His bed was gone and so was his dishes. Gram said he died. His time on earth was over with."

Meghan recalled her mother's explanation of the death of her cat, Chancey. The cat was almost twenty years old, and had been a part of the family since Meghan was about ten years old. The cat died a few

157

weeks before Meghan's abduction, and she struggled even then with attempting to explain the death to her daughter. She reached over the table and picked up her daughter's bowl, wondering what she might offer to make the thought of death easier for her daughter to understand.

"Well." Meghan walked to the sink, recalling the family cat sleeping in her bed when she was in middle school. The cat often provided Meghan comfort as it snuggled against her body to stay warm. Once, when Meghan was twelve years old, she had closed her door for privacy after a tough day at school. The young cat pressed against the door and meowed until Meghan let the cat enter her room.

Promptly, and without knowledge of Meghan's hardship, the cat found its place on the bed. As it nestled against Meghan's torso and began to purr, she smiled, realizing that the cat had no knowledge of her day at school. It provided unconditional love, regardless of the surroundings.

"Momma, are you crying because Chancey is dead?" Amanda asked as she stood beside Meghan, her hands raised high in the air.

As Meghan realized she was standing at the sink crying, she wiped the tears from her eyes and wondered.

Meghan dropped the bowl and yogurt cup into the sink and picked up her daughter. "Yes, sweetie. Chancey was a good cat and a great friend."

The answer came without thought or planning. "Sweetie, I suppose God decides. He decides when it's time for things to go up to heaven and live with him."

Amanda turned to her mother and placed her milk soaked hands onto her face. "Everything goes to heaven when it dies? Even Stephanie?"

Meghan, recalling the death of Amanda's gold fish Stephanie, pondered her response. She smiled and opted for the easy response, and as she did, she wondered exactly who did decide and how. "Yes, sweetie. All things go to heaven."

Meghan swallowed the small lump that rose in her throat.

"Even Stephanie."

CHAPTER TWENTY - ONE

FUCK IT.

YOU'RE GOING TO DIE ANYWAY.

TWENTY - ONE. What little interaction that Ryan had with Meghan allowed him, for the first time in his life, to *feel*. Now, filled with emotion, Ryan felt a certain depth within him that he had not experienced in his entire adult life. He felt as if his life had purpose. He now realized why people developed a love for a person that they were not bound to by the ties of family or blood. Ryan felt, although she was no longer in his presence, that Meghan had become an important part of his life.

A week prior, after a thorough survey of the land that surrounded the remote home, Ryan was certain that his plan *could* work. The home was positioned approximately two miles into the rural area that surrounded the city. The ten acres of land that surrounded the home allowed access from the front through the driveway leading to the house. The rear of the property was primarily pasture land surrounded by a fence with two gates that used as egress to the fenced acreage. A small pond was centered in the ten acre pasture.

Now sitting in his vehicle in the driveway, Ryan inhaled through his nose. A slow deep breath allowed a calmness to wash over him and provided him with assurance that he would be able to proceed.

Dressed in Khaki pants, a pressed khaki shirt, and boots, Ryan turned his head and looked along the rural road in front of the home. There wasn't another house within half a mile of the residence. It would be difficult, he assured himself, for anyone to hear or see what was about to happen.

He inhaled another breath through his nose and grabbed the door handle of the stolen van. As he exhaled slowly through his mouth, he pulled the handle and stepped from the van into the driveway. After double-checking the placement of his photo identification clipped to the light jacket he was wearing, he methodically walked up the drive toward the front door of the residence.

Standing on the porch, Ryan inhaled another shallow breath through his nose. As he held his breath, he pressed the button for the doorbell affixed beside the frame of the door. Eagerly, as he waited for the resident to answer the door, he exhaled and listened for any sign of movement in the home. After thirty seconds, he knocked on the door three times sharply.

As he heard the bolt in the door lock turning, Ryan began to feel relief. Planning any type of event and not being able to execute the plan never settled very well with him. As the door opened, Ryan gazed into the eyes of the resident and spoke clearly and with precision.

"Sir, I'm Blake Johnson with The Gas Service Company. Our systems have indicated a leak of forty-two cubic feet per hour at this residence. Although we are uncertain of the *exact* leak location, we're quite sure it is coming from this residence." Ryan motioned to each side of the front of the home. "I'll need to ask your permission to enter the residence and attempt to locate and repair the leak."

Based on the expression on the man's face, Ryan began to feel at ease.

The man grinned and opened the door. "Wow. Here? Shit. Yeah, by all means, come in."

Ryan pushed his hands deep into his pants pockets, stepped past the man, and into the living room of the home. "I appreciate your courtesy - especially this late at night. As this isn't the time of year that most homes consume natural gas, we made note of the leak right away. Can you direct me to the gas furnace and gas water heater, please?"

Ryan blinked his eyes and offered a false grin.

"Sure, follow me," the man said.

As the man walked toward the kitchen, Ryan reached under the tail of his Jacket and into the waistband of his pants. This practice measure provided enough reassurance for Ryan to become comfortable of his ability to retrieve the pistol from his waistband without effort or concern. After placing his hands into his front pockets again, he followed the man to the basement door located at the edge of the kitchen.

As the man began to walk down the stairs, Ryan paused. Without thought, he pulled his hands from his pockets and rubbed his palms on the thighs of his pants as the man worked his way to the bottom of the steps.

The man gazed up the steps and chuckled. Well, it's down here in the utility room, you're going to have to come down those steps."

"Sorry, I thought I was going to sneeze," Ryan lied.

He inhaled a deep breath and waited for enough courage to proceed. In a moment, the desire to complete his intended mission overcame his fear, and he began to walk down the steps.

As the man reached the basement, he turned to the left and disappeared from view. Ryan walked down the steps, reached the landing, and turned left around the wall that separated the stairs from the main body of the basement. In an illuminated room full of boxes and mechanical equipment the man stood waiting, his hands placed firmly on his hips.

The man stared at the water heater. "I don't smell a damned thing."

"You can't *always* smell them. The leaks, that is," Ryan assured him.

"It's why I brought the leak detector. It can detect a miniscule amount up to 50 parts per million – far below our nose's ability to determine any form of leak. Step aside please," Ryan said.

The man stepped to the side of the door and allowed Ryan to pass between him and the heater that stood beside the entrance of the door. As Ryan reached the rear of the heater – out of the man's view – he pressed the *test* button on the detector he had purchased at Home Depot an hour earlier. The detector beeped twice loudly, startling the man on the other side of the heater.

"Well, we have one small one right here. We may need to evacuate the home if there's many more. It's difficult to be too certain just yet. I guess now is the time to ask, is there anyone else in the home?" Ryan asked.

"No, I'm the only one that lives here," the man responded.

Standing on the opposite side of the heater, out of view of the man, Ryan placed his detector back into the belt clip. He removed the pistol from the waistband of his pants. Cautiously, he switched the safety off.

"You are the owner of the residence, are you not? Joshua Volvo?"

Out of view, Ryan raised the pistol and waited for a response.

"Yep, that's me," Josh responded from the other side of the heater.

"Two more places I need to check, just a minute." Ryan said. He stepped around the heater and into view.

Josh's eyes widened at what he saw. "What the fuck…"

164

Ryan pointed the barrel at the crotch of the Josh's jeans and pulled the trigger.

The explosion was deafening, and the concussion from the recoil of the pistol startled Ryan. Quickly, he recovered, pointing the pistol at Josh's chest. As he stood with the pistol at arm's length, Josh's legs gave out and he slowly lowered himself to the floor.

"Don't say a word, or I'll shoot you in the chest. I prefer not to listen to you at all, so be quiet if you don't mind. Whining has always irritated me," Ryan shouted.

Ryan licked the roof of his mouth in an effort to remove the taste of the cordite. The coppery smell of blood filled the air as Josh fell to the floor, groaning. As he sat on the floor, he continued to groan and press his hands into this lap.

Ryan knelt beside Josh and began to speak quietly.

"You see, I wanted to be certain to shoot you in the groin. I have no idea how that feels, but I suspect it isn't a great feeling. Am I correct? The detectives will look at the psychological aspect of it later. They'll assume you were disgusted with yourself, as you should be. Well, enough of that. You have no idea what I'm speaking of, and to be quite honest." Ryan paused and pressed his tongue against the roof of his mouth. "I am tired of looking at you and speaking to you already."

Ryan stood and looked around the room.

Josh shouted as he pushed his hands against his groin. Blood seeped through his fingers and onto the floor. "Oh lord, call me an ambulance."

Ryan glared at him.

"Come on, I need an ambulance."

Ryan pointed the pistol at Josh's temple. "Enough. Stop speaking. Listen, Mr. Volvo. I am here in an effort to send you to hell for what you have done to your niece, Meghan. You, Sir, disgust me."

"I need an ambulance," Josh begged.

"An ambulance?" Ryan Chuckled. "Fuck it, you're going to die anyway."

As Josh opened his mouth to plead further, Ryan pulled the trigger. The deafening sound filled the room. As the blood oozed from Josh's groin and head, Ryan placed the pistol in his waistband and removed his jacket.

He folded his jacket into a thick bundle and placed it on the floor on the right side of Josh. After placing the jacket on the floor, he reached into his front pocket and removed a pair of rubber gloves and one cartridge for the pistol. He placed the cartridge between his elbow and his torso, pressing it against his shirt. Carefully, he stretched the gloves over his hands and removed the pistol from his waistband and the cartridge from between his elbow and stomach.

After removing the magazine, he loaded the spare cartridge into the pistol. With his gloved hands, he wiped the pistol free of all fingerprints with his shirt. He then bent over, formed Josh's lifeless hand around the frame of the firearm, and pressed his finger into the trigger guard.

Cupping his gloved hand around Josh's hand, he pressed the barrel into the folded jacket, and pulled the trigger. Carefully placing Josh's bloody hand around the pistol, Ryan released Josh's arm and allowed it to fall naturally back into the location where it had been.

After picking up the jacket, discharged round, and one of the shell casings, Ryan stepped over the body and into the doorway. The detectives would now find two shell casings, and two discharged bullets, one in Josh's head, and one in his groin or hip. Josh's hand would be covered in gunpowder and blood, supporting the indication that he shot himself.

The amount of cartridges missing from the magazine of the pistol would precisely match the amount of bullets that were in Josh's body.

Two.

The suicide note would make the investigation relatively short.

In time, the detectives would potentially find more; potentially in a matter of weeks or even months. Either way, Meghan's mother would see Josh for who he was, and not at the telling of Meghan. Without a doubt, Meghan would feel relief from Josh's untimely demise.

He stepped over the body and around the corner of the basement, holding the jacket in his gloved hand. In entering the kitchen, Ryan removed his gloves and placed them on top of the jacket on the center of the floor. He pushed his hand deep into the pocket of his khaki pants and removed another pair of rubber gloves and pulled them over his sweaty hands.

He looked up from his glove covered hands and peered down the hallway of the house. He walked down the corridor to the rear of the home, and opened each of the doors independently. The first was a bathroom. The second, without a doubt, was Josh's bedroom, the third a spare bed room. He flipped the light switch and illuminated the spare bedroom. As he turned to face the foot of the bed, a sigh of relief passed his lips.

The typewriter.

What appeared to be a World War II era Smith-Corona.

Ryan began opening the drawers to the desk. He smiled as he peered into the lower right drawer and found a loose sheet of paper. After feeding the paper into the typewriter, he placed his gloved hand on his chin and thought. Methodically, he pressed the keys on the typewriter.

My disgust turned into shame, and the shame to pain.

The pain, now, is too much to fathom.
And with these parting words,
I become numb.

He read what he typed. A smile formed. He then reached into his rear pants pocket and retrieved a small zip-lock type bag and opened it. He reached into the bag and removed one of the post-mortem fingernail clippings from Shellie's fingers and dropped it on the floor. Satisfied at what was available for the detectives in this room, he turned and walked to the bathroom.

Ryan stepped into the bathroom, to the shower, and pulled the shower curtain open. Carefully, he removed a few of the strands of Elena's hair from the small plastic bag and dropped them in the bathtub. After tossing a few strands onto the floor, he stepped into the hallway pleased of his placement of clues.

As he walked down the hallway and toward the kitchen, he zipped the plastic bag and placed it into his rear pants pocket. After recovering the jacket and gloves from the kitchen, he walked to the van, opened the rear cargo doors, and placed his items in the rear of the van. As he walked to the front of the van he considered potential forgotten items. Convinced that he remembered everything of importance, he opened the door, got inside, and removed his gloves.

A sense of satisfaction filled Ryan as he started the van. He felt satisfied, in a somewhat sickening sense, that he and Meghan were now equal. Satisfied he had accomplished his goal, and satisfied that Meghan's abuser would not be capable of harming another.

Ryan backed the van out of the driveway, drove to the rural location where he had left his bicycle, and parked the van. After retrieving his bicycle from the fence it was locked to, he walked to the rear of the van and opened the cargo doors. A back pack and a can of gas sat inside the doors. He gathered his backpack, unzipped it, and removed his sneakers. He then removed his outer khaki shirt and boots, and placed them in the back pack with his jacket and gloves. After he laced up his sneakers, he zipped the backpack and stood up.

Ryan hung the backpack on the handlebars. As if he'd done it a hundred times, he walked back to the van, opened the driver's door and removed a pack of cigarettes and a book of matches from the glove compartment. He felt awkward lighting the cigarette, but fumbled through the process, knowing the night was close to being over. As the cigarette dangled from his lips, he puffed on it and walked to the rear of the van.

After placing the matches in his front pocket, he doused the interior of the van in gasoline and tossed the can inside the vehicle. Knowing that a cigarette alone wouldn't ignite the fuel, Ryan removed the book of matches from his pocket and folded the paper cover of the matches around the burning cigarette, leaving the glowing tip an inch from the head of the matches.

The cigarette would burn, and within about five minutes, it would reach the match heads. The temperature of the burning cigarette would then ignite the potassium chlorate in the match heads, and cause the book of matches to combust and burn. The gasoline fumes in the fuel soaked van would explode as soon as the cigarette caused the matches to ignite.

Carefully, he placed the burning cigarette and matches in the rear of the van and closed the door.

Without much effort, he would be two miles away by the time the van exploded. As he climbed onto the bicycle and secured the backpack, he realized that he was breathing without trying, without effort. The majority of the latter part of the evening, to him, was without thought.

As Ryan pedaled the bicycle toward his home, he began to realize that he felt no remorse for the killing. For now, all he felt was a form of resolution that he attributed to making the world a better place.

And he began to wonder.

In which direction his life was headed.

CHAPTER TWENTY - TWO

MOTHER, I HAVE A QUESTION.

TWENTY-TWO. "The bagels are multi-grain. I don't know the difference between those and whole wheat."

Ryan sighed as he sat down and looked out the window. "Mother, it's simple. Whole wheat bagels are prepared using whole wheat. Multi-grain are prepared using wheat as well as grains other than wheat. Multiple grains, mother."

"Are you pleased that I bought the cheese, Ryan?" his mother asked as she walked toward the table.

Ryan stared out the window at the flowers and smiled. His thoughts were elsewhere on this particular morning. There was no manner of living or doing that would change his past. Attempting to forget what had happened would certainly be his best step, he thought; but doing so had proven difficult at best. His knowledge of the human mind afforded him a very detailed understanding of what the future should hold in mental health. As he stared out the window, he wondered what he could become, at his best.

What he feared was also what he seemed to desire.

He gazed through the glass, realizing the agreement he made with the Japanese businessmen after his game ended in a debacle was going to be difficult to implement. His confidence in himself was slowly growing,

171

something he valued far more than the money he would possibly earn. The longer he studied the flowers, the more convinced he became that he could pull off the new plan.

He wanted more than anything to wash his hands of all of his memories of the events that were beginning to haunt him. The memories, oddly enough, weren't as much of the abductions and killing as they were of his father. Strangely, he felt that killing had become an option for many of life's difficulties, and he struggled with forcing himself to think otherwise. The events associated with the abduction seemed to allow him to forget his father's actions. Possibly, he finally decided, the killing made his father's behavior seem miniscule.

Once the human mind crosses the boundary of killing and processes the emotion associated with it, it often becomes a future desire. Continuing to kill allows the mind to believe the severity of killing isn't as great as it believed prior to the first killing taking place. Ryan knew this. The mind forcing the body to perform the act again, all in an effort to manipulate the brain to trust that killing was in fact not as heinous as it originally believed it to be. The result often produced serial killers and career criminals.

Ryan reached for his plate and realized that he had already eaten his entire bagel. He looked out the window and blinked, attempting to focus on the flowers. The flowers provided a level of solace that he could not find elsewhere.

"You're not even listening, Ryan," his mother complained.

He turned to face his mother as he spoke. It was important that he see her eyes as she responded. "Mother, I have a question."

She grinned and widened her eyes slightly.

"How aware were you of my abuse as a child?"

Ryan looked into his mother's eyes and waited for her to respond.

She shrugged nervously. "Well. I don't guess I know what you're asking."

Ryan cleared his throat. "Mother, listen. When I was a child, father used to take me into the basement and abuse me. I have always told myself that you didn't know. I wonder, however just what you *did* know."

He crossed his hands in his lap and relaxed as he waited for his mother to respond.

Her eyes moved up and to the right as she began to speak. Ryan, aware that she was right handed, knew that this indicated she was telling a lie. He watched her facial expressions as she spoke.

"Ryan, your father didn't abuse you. He took you to the basement and talked to you. He taught you important lessons. He raised you with a stern hand and your success is a result of that upbringing." Her shaking hands quickly moved to the coffee cup.

"Mother, stripping a child of his clothes and belittling him, telling him that God did not love him and that he was worthless is abuse in a grand degree. Do you disagree?"

Ryan felt relieved to be speaking of this to his mother after all of the years that had passed.

"Your father loves you, Ryan." She picked her cup up from the saucer and looked into it. She placed it back onto the saucer and turned to face the window. "Your father is a man of discipline, Ryan. His father was a man of discipline. You're a very disciplined man as a result."

She nodded in Ryan's direction. "Like father like son,"

Ryan felt as if his body temperature was beginning to rise. He detested thinking of becoming anything like his father. Desperately, he wanted to be different, to be normal, to be responsible for his successes and to *feel* successful. His financial endeavors had proven to him that his mind's perception of success did not lie in the form of monetary gains. It was merely a distraction and false form of satisfaction. A mask.

Desperately, he wanted to believe that his mother was not aware of what happened to him as a child. As he sat in the chair across from his mother, he began to wonder. Loyalties, devotion, love, and commitment came into question. As he turned to look out the window, he began to feel betrayed.

Ryan stood from his chair. "Mother, I am going to go now."

He looked down at his coffee cup and crumb covered plate, exhaled, and shook his head lightly.

"I'll tell your father you stopped…"

"Tell my father nothing," Ryan snapped, interrupting her mid-sentence.

As he stood on the porch, he drew a shallow breath, taking in the scent of the flowers. He turned his left wrist and looked at his watch. He stepped from the porch and walked toward the flower garden enjoying the sweet aroma with each step.

As he stood amidst the flowers, he smiled. Here, and only here, he was able to lose his sense of what was real. Here, as a child, he was able to come to believe that there was a being greater than himself. Here, he was able to relax. The smell of the flowers, to him, was proof of an existence of a higher power.

As he surveyed all of the flowers, one rose stood out as exceptional. Perfect. Symmetrical.

Blood red.

Ryan reached out and carefully plucked the rose from the bush. He raised the rose to his nose, closed his eyes, and inhaled. As he opened his eyes, he turned and looked down at his watch.

And he smiled.

CHAPTER TWENTY - THREE

REMEMBER ME?

TWENTY-THREE. The music played quietly as Meghan sat and sipped her coffee. Without thinking, she tapped her fingers on the top of the table to the beat of the music. After unsuccessfully attempting to identify the artist, she gave up and looked down at the magazine she was reading.

Ryan stepped beside the table where Meghan was seated. "It isn't every day that you hear *Heartless Bastards* playing in a public place. Is this seat taken?"

Meghan sighed upon recognizing the voice. "It. It's uhmm. It's free. It's open." She closed her magazine and set it aside.

"I want to apologize again, and ask if you'd like to talk. If not, I understand. This is a small city, and we'll certainly encounter one another from time-to-time, but I don't want to cross any…" Ryan had not finished his thought before Meghan interrupted him.

"I'd love to," Meghan blurted.

"Well, alright. I have a lot of things to say, and several to ask, Meghan. I saw you seated here as I ordered my coffee and I figured I'd see if you'd like to talk," Ryan lied.

Ryan had watched Meghan for almost a month prior to abducting her. This coffee shop was a place that she frequented while her daughter was at school. As today was the next to the last day of school, Ryan assumed Meghan may be having a cup of morning coffee. Pleased when he noticed her SUV in the parking lot, Ryan decided to come inside and act as if their meeting was happenstance.

"Well, first and foremost, I am sorry for how things unfolded." Ryan paused and looked toward the coffee bar.

Meghan sighed as she dropped the magazine into the container that sat beside her seat. "Let's get past that. Truthfully, I'd really rather just forget it. Tragedy. I'm so tired of the tragedy. I believe everything happens for a reason."

Ryan rubbed his chin and studied Meghan for a moment. Uncertain if his opinion of her changed for the right reason, he struggled with how he now felt. This was the first time they had spoken since he released her, and as he watched her and listened to her speak, he realized that he was attracted to her. The attraction made him feel uneasy. He raised his left leg, crossed it over his right knee, and placed his hands in his lap.

"Do you truly believe you'll be able to set it aside and move on, Meghan?" Ryan asked.

Meghan shrugged her shoulders and raised her eyebrows comically. After she lowered her shoulders, she felt guilty for making light of the situation, not knowing how Ryan truly felt about what had happened.

Ryan tossed his head toward the coffee bar. "My drink is ready. Do you want anything?"

"No thank you," Meghan responded.

Nervous, Meghan shifted in her seat. Without thinking, she raised her hands to her head and raked her fingers through her hair. As her fingers cleared her hair she shook her head, allowing it to fall onto her shoulders. As she rubbed the sweat from her palms and considered walking to the bathroom, Ryan pulled the seat away from the table and sat down.

"So, you believe everything happens for a reason?" Ryan asked.

Ryan raised his cup to his mouth and took a shallow drink.

Meghan watched Ryan's movements intently. "I do."

She studied Ryan's hands as he gripped his cup of coffee, intrigued by his use of hand gestures as he spoke. She felt nervous sitting across the table from him – the kind of nervous she felt in middle school when one of her girlfriends would tell her that a boy liked her. As Ryan placed his cup on the table and raised his hand to his face, Meghan smiled.

He tapped his index finger on his upper lip and gazed far beyond Meghan as he spoke. "I'll be candid, Meghan. I have become frustrated with life."

Meghan sighed. "What can I do to help?"

"Well, I am not certain. I have spent my adult life measuring my success by earning money and hoarding it, so to speak. Something happened during all of *that*." Ryan paused, still focused on the wall behind Meghan, uncertain of what to say regarding the events that tied him and Meghan together. "Things seem so different now. I have *other* concerns. I want to proceed with life. Move on. Maybe I just want to feel *clean*. I don't know. I know this, I need a change."

Ryan's eyes fell from his point of focus.

He raised his hand to his chin, turned, and studied Meghan's face.

Meghan examined Ryan's posture, and admired his handsome looks. As he reached for his coffee, she watched his hand. Her mouth curled into a smile. As she looked back up at his face, she opened her mouth to speak and mentally struggled with her choice of subjects.

"Do you think about it?" she asked.

He nodded. "It's *all* I think about. I am incapable of stopping. I fill my days with events and try refrain from thinking all together. And you?"

"From time to time I think about it. I don't know, it's probably not as bad as it could be. I try to convince myself it never happened," she said.

She paused as she admired Ryan's choice of clothing.

Meghan chuckled as she motioned toward him with her open hand. "I wish we had met under different circumstances, I suppose. Oh, and do you always dress like this?"

"The circumstances we met under," he said. "They prevent us from having anything normal between us, don't they? And yes, as a matter of fact, I always dress like this."

Ryan had no expectation of having anything develop with Meghan, but he had hope. Desperately, now more than ever, he wanted to attempt to live a normal life. His mind filled with events and emotion that he didn't care to think about, he waited for her to respond. Nervously, he uncrossed his legs, and crossed the right leg over his left knee.

Meghan smiled. "Actually no they don't. I have no idea why I feel this way, and I have hoped you or someone could enlighten me. I don't look at what happened as preventing me from *anything* with you. I imagine you're going to tell me what's wrong with me or why I should think differently, but I don't."

She raised her hands, waiting for Ryan to give her a diagnosis in supporting her feelings of desire toward him.

Ryan uncrossed his legs and sat forward in his chair, placing his hands on his knees. Excitedly, he began to speak.

"So, let me get this straight." he paused and rubbed his hands on his thighs. "You have zero concern regarding seeing me, talking to me, or attempting to potentially develop further depth to a relationship?"

She brushed her hair from her face and folded it over her ear. "I'm not sure what you just asked me, but I'll answer with what I *feel*. I would hang out with you and see what happened. Nothing that has occurred in the past would prevent us from proceeding with *anything*. I'm attracted to your personality and I find you extremely attractive."

Ryan sat back in his chair and crossed his left leg over his right knee. He studied Meghan's face, admiring her facial features and clear skin. As he watched her he began to consider all of the reasons he shouldn't consider attempting any form of relationship with Meghan. In coming to meet her, it wasn't his intent to attempt to develop a relationship, but to find a means of convincing himself that what happened wasn't as bad as it seemed to be. Potentially using Meghan as a manner of resolve.

He leaned forward and grabbed his beverage from the table. As his hand formed around the cup, he realized the temperature had dropped considerably. Concerned with the passage of time, instinctively, he looked at his watch.

"Do you need to leave?" Meghan asked.

"Actually, no. I do not. I was concerned with your need to pick up your daughter," he responded.

She glanced at the clock on the wall behind him. "Oh, not for an hour and a half."

The thought of developing *anything* with Meghan began to interest Ryan greatly.

"I see, well let's continue this by all means," Ryan said.

"I have a question I have been meaning to ask. I found you on that dating site, Plenty of Fish. How can someone of your intelligence, striking good looks, and magnetic personality be single? You certainly have hundreds of potential dates from the sight, do you not?" Ryan asked.

Meghan sat forward in her seat, eager to offer her answer to him. The thought of something between her and Ryan becoming *real* began to fill her. She had no understanding for why she felt the way she felt about him, but she didn't care to. Concerned more with *how* she felt, and not *why* she felt the way she did, she offered her explanation.

"Well, I started that about two months ago. I decided I would try and whittle the potential partners down to a select few, and when Amanda started school next year, I would go on a few dates. My desires for a partner are, well." Meghan hesitated, feeling a little uncomfortable with what she wanted to say.

Ryan's eyes widened. "Your desires are?"

He rubbed his palms on his knees and anxiously waited for Meghan's response.

Meghan considered telling him the truth. She and her husband had divorced for several reasons, the primary being her sexual desires. Her former husband could say whatever he preferred to say about having a family, but she knew how things changed after she made her desires clear. She considered telling Ryan, and also contemplated lying.

Ultimately, she hoped he would understand her desires.

Her eyes fell to Ryan's feet. "I prefer things sexually that are not normal."

Ryan pressed his palms into his pants, attempting to dry his now uncomfortably wet hands. As he wiped his hands, he mouth formed a smile. He had yet to be with a woman sexually, and to his best recollection, had expressed this fact to Meghan. His desires, his fantasies, and his hope would be to have a woman who had sexual desires that were borderline BDSM.

The thought of sex that included bondage and light torture was very satisfying to him.

Ryan leaned into his chair, raising the front legs from the floor, and rocked the chair onto the rear legs. As the chair balanced, he smiled. His exposure to people included his mother and Ami, for the most part. There were several familiar faces throughout the city, but included primarily people he encountered at the car dealership, grocery store, and other establishments that he frequented. Having a conversation like this, to Ryan, was a tremendous pleasure. He decided to lure Meghan into a more detailed response.

Ryan chuckled. "Continue, please. Be more definitive. My sexual fantasies borderline criminal behavior."

Immediately, Meghan felt relief. The relief was followed by desire and arousal. As she felt herself become sexually stimulated, she adjusted herself in her seat. As she moved, she became more aroused. The thought of Ryan being sexually attracted to her wants and desires formed a smile on her face. Attempting to hide her satisfaction, she lightly covered her mouth with her hand.

As she considered her response, her clit began to tingle.

"Well. I *was* married. I expressed my desires to my husband and within a year or so, we were divorced. There were other things that I am sure contributed, and maybe it's just some weird guilt I feel, but I believe that he divorced me because he thought I was weird. Well, weird sexually," she said.

"You didn't answer the question," Ryan said flatly.

Meghan wiggled in her seat, looked up at the clock, and realized she had one more hour to spare. Again, she considered telling Ryan her wildest desire. As she changed her focus from the clock to Ryan, she noticed his relaxed posture and slight smile. Her thoughts became more sexual oriented and detailed. She began to fantasize about Ryan sexually, and wanted to tell him what her thoughts included. After all, he had asked for her to respond and be truthful. She sat up in her seat, leaned forward, and cupped her hand beside her mouth. As Meghan leaned forward, Ryan lowered his chair to the floor.

"I want to be tied up, maybe handcuffed. Tied up and talked dirty to. Blindfolded, that kind of stuff," Meghan whispered.

"During the course of sex, or just in general?" Ryan asked, intrigued.

Feeling more comfortable at Ryan's lack of rejection, Meghan cupped both hands over her mouth, leaned closer to Ryan, and continued.

"Oh, no. Sexually, I want tied up, blindfolded, slapped around, and treated like a slut. I want rough sex. *Really* rough sex. I don't know how rough, because I've never been there. But my fantasy is pretty brutal. I suppose if it ever happened I would know fairly quickly," she whispered.

As she spoke, she became aroused.

Uncomfortable aroused.

She shifted in her seat and attempted to find comfort. Her throbbing clit and soaking wet pussy prevented complete comfort, but the annoyance was welcomed.

Ryan sat, listened, and considered Meghan's statement. His knowledge regarding the human mind, his training in psychology, and his understanding of people allowed him to understand that some, if not all of Meghan's desires, came from her abuse as a child at the hand of her uncle. Additionally, he knew that his desire to be controlling came from his abuse at the hand of his father. Ryan quickly realized he and Meghan's sexual longings would be well suited for one another.

"Well, it makes perfect sense, psychologically speaking. Considering

184

your past, it's not abnormal, and in fact, it's quite healthy," Ryan said rather clinically.

Meghan sat back in her seat and sighed. Her mouth curled into a smile. She chuckled at the fact that she felt no guilt regarding her thoughts, and decided to reveal her slight pleasure.

"My uncle. They found him dead. Suicide. I hate to say it, but I have never felt better. I have no idea how I *should* feel, but I felt immediate relief. Like this huge weight I had carried my entire life was lifted from my chest." Meghan sighed, relieved for having spoken how she felt to *someone*.

Ryan attempted to look surprised. He wondered after killing her uncle how she would digest it. In time, if the bodies of the other women were found in the pond, her uncle would be believed to be guilty for the murders of Shellie and Elena. Meghan, however, would then know that Ryan was, at minimum, a participant in setting her uncle up on that portion of the crime. Momentarily, he considered the option of attempting to remove the bodies from the pond, and dismissed it as not being possible.

Ryan locked the fingers of his hands together and raised his folded hands to his face. "I am truly sorry for your loss, Meghan. Well, to as much of a degree is possible. The relief you feel is normal. It's closure. The feelings that you feel, from a professional standpoint, is quite healthy. You're beginning to heal subconsciously. You see him as being punished for the act, and you feel satisfied."

"Well." Meghan rotated her head from side to side and looked around her. "I kind of feel a guilty pleasure about it. I smiled when I heard."

Ryan began to think of his father and the hatred he felt regarding what he had done to him as a child. Ryan was aware of all of his own shortcomings as an adult, and attributed all of his faults and idiosyncrasies to his father. Right or wrong, Ryan blamed his father for each and every concern he had with himself as an adult. As he sat and thought, he began to become uncomfortable. He rotated his right hand, looked at his index finger, and his hatred mounted.

Ryan leaned forward and picked his coffee cup from the table. "I often think of my father, and what relief I would feel if he died. Most victims of child abuse feel a tremendous relief when their abuser dies. Confrontation and death are the two largest means of the victim feeling closure. I try desperately not to hate, Meghan, but I will confide in you. I hate that man for what he did."

Meghan thought of the lifetime she had spent feeling uneasy about her uncle. Her guilt, shame, concerns with exposure, and her desire for him to be punished. She considered how she felt now, and wished that Ryan could feel the same relief. For a fleeting moment, she considered what may change in Ryan if his father was dead. She expected Ryan would feel the same relief as she did.

Meghan glanced up at the clock, startled at the amount of time that had passed.

"This is so strange. We've been sitting here for an hour and a half talking like we're old friends. Again, call me weird, but I like it," She said. "I'm going to have to go, I need to be at the school in just a little bit."

Ryan stood. "So…"

Meghan did not feel threatened by Ryan in the least; and in fact, felt an odd comfort around him. Excited about the thought of Ryan becoming interested in her, their sexual interests being similar, and potentially having some sort of a sexual relationship with Ryan, Meghan interrupted Ryan as he spoke.

"Well, I'm thinking. I want to pick up Amanda, take her to my mother's for the afternoon, and see you. What do you think about that? Is that possible?" Meghan asked excitedly as she stood from her chair.

"Certainly," Ryan said with a smile.

Let me give you my phone number," he said. "And I'll clean up this mess."

And as he gave Meghan his phone number, he began to consider if he could truly clean up the potential mess that could be made of the bodies that were at the bottom of her uncle's pond. As he watched Meghan walk to the door he wondered if it even mattered. Although Meghan's admittance of wanting him sexually hadn't aroused him, as Meghan walked away, his plan for her caused him to become uncomfortably hard.

And he smiled.

CHAPTER TWENTY - FOUR

UNLEASHING THE BEAST.

TWENTY- FOUR. Nervously, Ryan pulled his car into the driveway and turned off the engine. He leaned over and removed the single rose from the cup of water that he obtained from the coffee shop. As he reached for the door handle, he drew a slow breath through his nose. He then opened the door, stepped from the car, looked up the sidewalk toward the porch, and exhaled.

He walked to the porch. With each step came wonder of the unknown. His apprehension had grown with each passing minute as the afternoon progressed. Part of him wanted for what may develop between him and Meghan to flourish.

By and large, however, he knew that it never could or would.

As he stepped in front of the front door, he leaned forward and pressed the doorbell button. As he waited, he inhaled a slow breath through his nose.

She opened the door.

Dressed in a light blue sun dress and flat sandals, Meghan stood in the doorway. Her hair pulled back in a ponytail, she looked considerably different than she had at the coffee shop. Ryan shifted his gaze from her face to her feet and back up to make eye contact with her as he held the rose at arm's length.

"I chose it for the symmetry and color," Ryan said.

Meghan smiled and accepted the rose. She then stepped aside, making room for Ryan to enter. "It's beautiful, thank you,"

Ryan nodded and smiled.

"My daughter's at my mother's for the week. Just so you know," Meghan offered as Ryan stepped into the house

As Ryan entered the hallway, Meghan began to walk toward the living room. Naturally, Ryan followed, observing the contents of the home as he did, admiring the simplicity of the Meghan's choice of decoration. As Meghan stepped in front of the couch, turned and sat down, Ryan stood and stared – uncertain of where he should sit.

Meghan leaned into the cushion of the couch and smelled the rose. "Sit in the chair if it makes you feel more comfortable."

Attempting to act comfortable, but feeling quite awkward, Ryan lowered himself into the chair at the corner of the living room and faced the couch. "So, it's three o' clock now. It will be dinner time soon. Would you like to eat together this evening?"

She nodded. "Maybe. I mean if you really want to. Or I can make something here if we get hungry."

Meghan stood from her seat. As she stood, Ryan pressed his hands into the arms of the chair and began to stand.

"No, stay comfortable. I'm just going to take this to the kitchen and put in in a vase of water. I'll be right back. Would you like something to drink?" she asked.

"No thank you."

As Meghan turned and stepped from the room, Ryan admired her physical features and the fit of her dress. As she walked away from him, he watched the shape of her butt rise and fall through the rear of her dress with each step. The anticipation of something developing sexually between them began to arouse him as she disappeared into the kitchen.

Sitting in the chair waiting, Ryan began to recall what he had seen on-line regarding BDSM sexual scenes. Although he had not physically been with a woman, he had experience at watching the sexual acts between men and women, his focus being BDSM, bondage, and forceful sexual acts. As his mind began to think of Meghan and his involvement with her, he became more aroused and less aware of his surroundings.

"I brought you a bottle of water," she said.

Startled, Ryan sat up in his chair and began to cross his legs. As he attempted to cross his left leg over his right, he realized he had reached full erection. Immediately, he uncrossed his legs and pressed his knees together. The boxer shorts and slacks he wore provided little if any support for hiding the fact that he was excited, erect, and emotionally ready.

Nervously, he looked up at Meghan.

"I uhmm. Well. Uhmm. Thank you," he stammered.

She placed the bottle of water on the table beside Ryan's chair. "Are you alright?"

Meghan, feeling sorrow for what she believed to be Ryan's uneasy and somewhat nervous nature, noticed his erection as she turned to face him. She considered sitting on the couch, and instead, knelt on the floor beside the front of the chair.

Meghan twisted the lid from her bottle of water. "So, what do you think could develop between us?"

Nervous, Ryan sat forward in his chair, felt immediate discomfort from his erection, and relaxed back into the rear of the seat. As he slumped into the seat, he glanced at his crotch, which now pointed straight up.

"I suppose." He turned to remove his bottle of water from the table. "That anything is possible. If what you said at the coffee shop was accurate."

She glanced at his crotch, shifted her eyes to meet his, and cocked an eyebrow. "Quite. Actually, I don't think I can emphasize it enough. I'm attracted to you. In some weird, sick probably borderline insane way, I feel I can be in a relationship with you without much effort at all."

"Why do you say in an insane, sick way? What do you mean?" he asked.

She wanted to unzip his slacks, pull out his cock, and force it down her throat until her eyes watered. She wanted to feel the pain from him attempting to make her choke on it. She wanted covered in his semen, covered in welts, and possibly even covered in his urine. She wanted to be slapped, beaten, and humiliated.

She feared, however, being completely honest in her desires. Instead of speaking her mind's thoughts, she spoke in generalities.

"Well, you kidnapped me, threatened me with murder, involved me in some weird-ass conspiracy, and had me kill someone to prove to you I wasn't going to go to the law about all of it," she said. "And, after all of that, I want to be with you. You're the Psychiatrist, tell me if that's normal."

She smiled and pressed the bottle between her legs, purposely raising the bottom of her dress up her thighs.

His eyes fell to Meghan's thighs. "*Psychologist*, and no. I suppose it's not. How we feel is how we feel. Changing it is often impossible. Figuring it out, at times, is almost as difficult."

"So, you've never been with a woman? No sex, no head, no making

192

out?" she asked.

He shook his head as she spoke.

"Anything?" Kissing?" she asked.

Somewhat embarrassed, Ryan shook his head and tipped the bottle to his mouth. As he drank from the bottle, Meghan leaned forward. The neck of her dress opened as she did, revealing the top of her bra. He swallowed hard and stared. As he attempted to shift his gaze and cross his legs, he realized his erection had become rather uncomfortable.

Meghan, sitting on the floor at the corner of the chair, shifted her weight to the other side of her butt and pulled her feet to meet her upper thighs. As she did, she purposely pulled her dress a little higher on her thigh, revealing more of her tanned legs for Ryan to view.

"Can I speak freely?" Meghan asked as she shifted her weight and leaned her upper body toward the chair.

Ryan, still nervously holding the water bottle close to his mouth and staring, nodded.

Meghan scooted across the floor, inching her way closer to the chair. "I want to suck your cock. I want to do that for you. I think it will loosen you up. Let me suck your cock."

"I uhhm. I hadn't really planned on us starting anything quite this early. We, uhhm. We barely know each other," Ryan stammered.

Meghan chuckled. "You kidnapped me, held me captive, and made me murder a woman in cold blood. Let me suck your cock, we'll call it even."

Ryan felt both uneasy and relieved that Meghan was comfortable laughing about the events that led to this. Her ability to joke about the murder could simply be her denial that the event happened; or she could, in his professional opinion, be consciously repressing the memory. As he struggled with thoughts of Meghan's placement of the memories, Meghan reached into his lap and toward his belt.

Ryan shifted in his seat as Meghan reached for his belt. "I, uhhm."

Meghan grinned. "Shhhh."

Ryan, although anxious, began to feel more comfortable as Meghan unbuckled his belt and unzipped his pants. Eagerly, he watched as her hand reached into his pants, through his boxers, and wrapped around his erection. As she pulled the tip of his cock upward, he flinched.

"Sorry, I can't get it out of here. It's as hard as a rock."

He gasped. "Your hands. They're cold."

Her eyes widened as her fingers wrapped around Ryan's stiff shaft. "Oh God. You have a gorgeous cock."

With her eyes fixed on Ryan's erection, Meghan raised her butt from the floor and knelt at the edge of the chair on her knees. She watched intently as his eyes followed her every movement. She reached with her left hand and grabbed her ponytail, flipping it over her left shoulder.

"Grab my hair."

Without speaking, Ryan reached for her ponytail, and held it tightly in his right hand – gripping it at the base of her skull. As he watched Meghan extend her tongue and lick the tip of his cock, he shivered.

"Does that feel good?" she asked.

As Ryan watched, he immediately began to feel more comfortable with Meghan, her desires, and his own. Attempting to recall everything he had witnessed in internet streaming videos, his mind began to become jumbled with practices, positions, and what to possibly say. As he drew a slow breath, he sat up in the chair and rolled his shoulders.

Meghan's gaze shifted to Ryan's eyes as she sat forward and began to wrap her lips around the tip of his cock. As her mouth encompassed the head fully, she closed her eyes and slid her lips half way down the shaft.

As Ryan's thickness filled her mouth, her mind began to wander to thoughts of him fucking her pussy, pounding her hard from behind. It had been years since she had had sex with anyone, and she was now well beyond being aroused. As her mouth slid up the shaft, she opened her eyes and glanced up at Ryan's face. As she shifted her knees, she felt her juices dripping onto her thighs. Her thoughts migrated to Ryan fucking her as she closed her eyes softly and began to slide her mouth down the thick shaft of Ryan's cock.

As Meghan's mouth worked its way up and down, she felt him began to rise from the seat. She opened her eyes, only to find him shifting his weight in the seat and bracing himself to stand. As his legs straightened, she extended her legs simultaneously.

"Open your mouth." He gripped her ponytail in one hand and her jaw in the other.

She stared back at him.

"Wide, Meghan. Open it wide," he demanded.

His pants fell to his ankles. He released her jaw and pressed his palm against the waistband of his boxers, pressing them along his thighs. Meghan looked up into Ryan's eyes, confused.

"Open your fucking mouth, Meghan," he demanded.

He gripped her jaw firmly in his hand. As she shifted her eyes to meet his, her lips pursed lightly. She wondered if what she felt she wanted and what she truly wanted were the same.

"Your mouth Meghan, open it. Don't make me tell you again," he growled.

As Meghan opened her mouth, Ryan forced his cock past her lips, causing her to gag as the tip pressed against her throat. As her eyes began to water, she instinctively raised her hands to her cheeks.

He released her jaw and slapped her hands away. "Keep your hands at your sides. Don't raise them again."

Meghan blinked her eyes and attempted to open her mouth further, allowing Ryan to force himself deeper into her throat. Ultimately, she wanted to please him.

Ryan's fingers reached for her upper neck. As he began to force himself in and out of her mouth, he gripped her neck tight in his hand. After a short time of forcing himself into her throat, he felt a pop, and his entire length slid into her throat.

He felt himself through the skin of her neck.

Meghan watched as his hips thrust close to her face. He grinned as he buried himself deep in her throat. As she fought to breathe, she began to question if this was in fact his first sexual encounter. He seemed, she thought, far too as ease with everything. Hoping to satisfy him, she closed her eyes and pressed her tongue against the shaft of his thick cock, making the passage into her throat easier to access.

More than anything, Meghan wanted to please Ryan's sexual desires.

He continued to moan, savagely fucking her throat. Saliva poured from her mouth and along her jaw, dripping down her neck. Her mascara ran from her eyes and along her cheeks, making the entire even seem slightly more morbid.

Ryan pressed his fingers into the back of Meghan's neck and his thumbs against her lower jaw. As he continued to force his entire length in and out of her mouth, she coughed and gagged.

His thumbs pushed harder against her jaw, forcing her head to tilt back. Aggressively, he forced himself into her throat. As she choked and coughed, he pressed further, until his scrotum was against her lower lip.

"You like that cock down your throat, you trashy little slut?" he asked.

Her mouth full of cock and her neck strained from Ryan's grasp, Meghan attempted to nod her head. As she realized she wasn't capable of overcoming the strength of Ryan's forearms, she blinked her eyes and mumbled against his thick shaft.

"Mmmm….mmmm," Megan sputtered as her saliva ran along her neck.

"You little whore."

His words aroused her further.

"You like being face fucked, don't you?"

She moaned.

"I should cover you in come. You're a filthy little slut. Filthy little sluts need covered in come."

Her pussy tingled. Her nipples ached. Again, she moaned.

The sound of his cock against the back of Meghan's throat, the moaning and whimpers as he forcefully fucked her mouth caused Ryan to become more excited. As the excitement began to heighten, he wanted more. The elevated euphoria he was feeling compared to what he felt from killing Meghan's uncle. As he forced her head back and pressed his cock hard against her throat, his target of satisfaction began to move.

Ryan was becoming bored.

He pulled himself from her mouth. As the tip of his dick cleared her lips, he slapped her face with tremendous force, catching her off-guard. The slap almost drove her to her knees.

"Stand up, you little slut."

Ryan's voice was deep and confident as he released Meghan's neck from his grasp.

As soon as Ryan's hands released her neck, his right hand gripped her pony tail and pulled her to her feet.

She whimpered.

His eyes widened. As he held her hair firmly in his hand, he slapped her again.

"I said *stand up*. When I speak, you listen. Do you understand me, slut?" Ryan barked.

Meghan was confused, excited, and not quite understanding exactly who this person was that stood before her. As she straightened her legs, she felt pain in her knees. As she pressed her palms to her thighs and stood, Ryan pulled her hair sharply, forcing her to stand completely erect.

"Oh *fuck*," Meghan gasped.

With his right hand gripping her ponytail, Ryan pulled Meghan's head toward his face. His left hand cupped around her neck and under her jaw, squeezing tightly.

He curled his arm, pulling her into him as he choked her. Now standing behind her with his chest pressed tight to her back, he rested his chin on his right wrist and breathed into her right ear.

"You little slut. You can't suck a cock to save your life. I should just choke your ass to death right now and do us both a little favor," Ryan growled.

"No, please," Meghan pleaded.

Ryan's hot breath caused Meghan to shiver. The forceful nature of the sex, the not knowing what was going to happen next, and the lack of planning this sexual escapade was exactly what Meghan had always fantasized about. Her pulse now elevated, she could feel her heartbeat against Ryan's hand as it squeezed her neck firmly.

She closed her eyes, pressed her feet into the floor, and leaned forward.

Meghan wanted to resist.

"You skinny little slut. You can't escape me," he growled. "You're going to get what you deserve."

He kicked his shoes across the floor.

His hand slid from Meghan's throat to under her dress. As he pressed his hand into her bra and squeezed her breasts, Meghan's eyes rolled and she released an audible sigh. Ryan widened his stance behind Meghan.

"You like that, you filthy bitch?" Ryan whispered as he pulled Meghan's hair, forcing the back of her head against his upper chest.

Ryan began walking forward, toward the couch where Meghan was seated earlier. Pushing against her as he walked, Ryan shoved Meghan forcefully, causing her to stumble as she stepped. As he squeezed her breasts and pulled her hair with tremendous force, Meghan began to whine.

"Please, be careful. What are you going to do to me?" Meghan whimpered.

Meghan had no understanding of what was going to happen next. The elevated excitement, forceful nature, and Ryan's deep demanding voice caused a level of sexual arousal that Meghan had never experienced. Her pussy was soaked. Now standing in front of the couch with Ryan's chest against her back, she could feel his cock through the material of her dress, pressing against the inside of her thigh.

Ryan's knees pressed against the back of her legs, causing her knees to bend. As she did, he pulled her hair harder.

"Pull your dress up over your ass, you whore," Ryan growled into her ear.

Nervously, Meghan fumbled to find the hem of her dress. As her hands bunched up the fabric, she eagerly raised it above her waist. As she did, Ryan removed his hand from her breast and slid it to her neck, squeezing firmly and pulling the back of her head to meet his face.

Ryan pressed his lips against the back of her neck and breathed into her ear. "I'm going to stuff your little wet pussy full of cock, Meghan. Do you know why?"

She fumbled to find the words. "I…I…I don't. Uhhm. I. No. Why?"

"Because I can. And you can't stop me. You don't want to stop me," he said. "Because you're a whore."

Her level of arousal was at an all-time high.

"And I want to feel what it's like to fuck you," he growled.

"Before I kill you."

Ryan slid his hand from the front of Meghan's neck to the back of her head. Pressing against her back with his chest, he caused her to bend at the waist as he forced her head into the cushions of the couch. His hips now pressing against her butt, he forced her head between the arm of the couch and the seat cushion. With his right hand holding her head in place, he grabbed her panties with his left hand and pulled sharply, snapping the fabric in two.

As Meghan felt Ryan's cock penetrate her, she groaned into the couch cushion. Her slight fear and uncertainty cast aside, she grunted with each thrust of his hips. The sounds of their skin slapping together became hypnotic as Ryan's hand pressed harder against the back of her head. Meghan labored with breathing as he continued to forcefully fuck her.

As she felt her pussy begin to contract, she moaned into the cushion of the couch.

As he pounded his cock deep inside her pussy, Meghan fought to breathe and moaned in ecstasy; reaching a degree of climax she had never known.

Ryan lifted his right foot from the floor and raised it onto the couch. With his left foot on the floor, and his right foot beside Meghan's head, he released his grasp of her head with his hand.

Meghan attempted to raise her head from the couch, but he stopped her short, stepping on her neck with his foot. He pressed her face into the void between the cushion and the arm of the couch, grinding the arch of his foot onto the base of her skull.

With one foot on the floor and one on Meghan's neck, Ryan began to fuck her harder and harder. The entry of his thick shaft into her soaking wetness was now easier and without any obstruction.

With each stroke, a muffled grunt could be heard from the couch cushions.

"Holy fuck, that cock is deep now, isn't it?" Now *that*, Meghan, is balls deep. You feel my balls against your wet little pussy?" Ryan grunted.

Ryan extended his right leg, using his thigh muscles to press his foot against Meghan's neck with more force. As his foot slid up her neck and onto the back of her head, he pressed down with his harder, smashing Meghan's face into the frame of the couch. As he pushed against her head, he continued to force his cock in and out of her pussy and scream as he did so.

"Fuck, Meghan. I think I might just cum," Ryan bellowed.

Meghan fought to breathe.

"Yes, I'm sure of it," Ryan assured her.

Methodically, Ryan continued to fuck her with long harsh strokes. With his left foot between her feet, and his right pressing against her head, each stroke was penetrating as deep as possible. With his upper thigh against Meghan's lower back, he pressed his cock as deep as he could and held it deep inside of her.

Meghan's body began to shudder and shake. From her pussy to her nipples, she felt as if she was being shocked. She had never experienced anything like this before, and was incapable of expressing her feelings. The darkness of her head being buried by Ryan's foot was amplified by the force in which Ryan was pressing against her head. As Ryan held his cock buried deep inside of her, everything she was able to see went black and her ears began to ring.

"Oh fuck, Meghan. Here it comes," Ryan howled.

As Meghan reached the height of her orgasm, she felt Ryan's cock begin to swell. As he pulled it from deep inside of her, she sighed and relaxed as best she could. As she felt his hands spread her ass cheeks apart, she tensed her arms and stomach muscles. Almost immediately, she heard Ryan groan and felt the warm spurts of cum against her ass.

Ryan released the pressure of his foot from Meghan's head. Slowly, she began to raise her head from the couch. As she did, she felt Ryan's hand on her right shoulder, lifting her from the awkward position.

As she stood, her legs shook and her knees began to wobble.

Ryan extended his arms around her back and under her armpit, holding her from falling.

"Here, let me help you to the bathroom," Ryan whispered as he held the weight of her body against his right arm.

As he turned toward the hallway, Meghan's legs gave out. Exhausted, and in a heightened state of euphoria, she was incapable of walking. As her legs failed, Ryan reached under her thighs with his left arm and picked her up from the floor.

"Carrying you might be easier," Ryan chuckled as he hoisted Meghan from the floor.

Meghan sighed. "Holy fuck. First time, huh?"

"Excuse me?"

"Your first sex. That was it?"

"Oh. Yes. That was my first time doing it. I'm fascinated with watching it, though. I just did what I've seen others do," Ryan admitted.

Standing at the entrance of the bathroom, Ryan stood and admired Meghan's attractive features. As she removed her dress, bra, and jewelry, her hands shook uncontrollably. Standing before him naked, Meghan's body appeared much younger than her almost thirty years of age. Ryan, still dressed in his shirt, unbuttoned it and set it on top of the bathroom vanity.

He watched as she reached into the shower and turned on the water. The emotion he felt from the aggressive sex was comparable to the excitement and satisfaction he felt from killing Meghan's uncle and watching her kill Elena. Consciously, as he watched Meghan step into the shower, he compared the two events and his feelings associated with both.

"Are you going to get in with me?" Meghan asked.

Ryan, feeling somewhat disconnected from reality, nodded his head lightly. He turned to focus on Meghan, trying to make sense of the situation. His life, he began to feel, had become a whirlwind of changes. Changes he felt he wasn't necessarily prepared for or could prepare for.

As he watched the water from the shower raining down on Meghan's naked body, he realized that he was not the failure his father had told him he would be.

"Well, get in here. Water is going everywhere," Meghan laughed as she motioned toward the bathroom floor.

As Ryan stepped into the shower, he thought of his torturous father, of Meghan, and of yet more murder.

And his mouth slowly curled into a smile.

CHAPTER TWENTY - FIVE

HEY BUDDY, NEED A RIDE?

TWENTY - FIVE. With his shoulders held high, chin tilted up slightly, and his hair freshly trimmed, Ryan maintained a level of confidence he had never felt. As he walked toward the entrance of the coffee shop, he noticed Ami standing at the cash register.

Ami smiled. "Hi, Ryan."

"Good evening," Ryan responded.

"Your hair looks nice; did you just get it cut?" Ami asked.

Ryan stood on the other side of the countertop, looking at the overhead beverage menu. He nodded his head and momentarily raised his eyebrows jokingly. "They say the best haircut is one that is never noticed."

Ryan chuckled.

"The usual?" Ami asked.

"No, I think I want something new," Ryan responded.

"Wow. Ok. Well, do you want something sweet, salty, healthy, more of a coffee taste, chocolate?"

"I'm not certain. Something *different*."

"I didn't figure you as a man for making too many changes."

"Well, I'm making changes in my life, and my first change is the willingness to make change."

"How about a Chai tea latte," he said.

She nodded. "Perfect, I think you'll love it."

He handed her a ten-dollar bill. "I was surprised to see you here this late at night. Surely you don't work morning shift and night shift both."

"Oh, yeah. We have a new manager. They promoted me to night shift lead. Actually, it works better with my school schedule."

"Put the change in the tip jar, Ami," he said.

He turned and looked over the seating are for a place to sit, surprised that the coffee shop was practically empty.

Ryan walked to a table and sat down as he waited for his drink to be prepared. He watched as Ami wiped the countertop, and day dreamed about what her sexual desires may be. Recalling the events of the night with Meghan caused him to smile and chuckle to himself as he imagined tying Ami to the posts of his bed and pouring hot wax over her naked body.

"Ryan, your drink is ready," Ami shouted across the coffee shop.

Ryan stood and walked to the coffee bar to receive his drink. As he walked past Ami, she brushed her hair with her hand, momentarily exposing the tattoo beside her ear. As Ryan reached for his coffee, he wondered if there was any statistical data to support his belief that women with tattoos were more prone to be sexually adventurous. He had always believed that they were, but now realized that his opinion was unfounded.

"So, are you headed home?" Ami asked as Ryan walked past the cash register.

Ryan nodded as he reached for his drink. "Yes, as a matter of fact."

He grabbed his drink from the bar and turned to face Ami. Full of confidence and a newly fueled sexual desire, the words escaped his mouth before he realized that his mind intended for him to speak. "If I were single, available, and asked you out on a date, would you consider going?"

He took a sip of his beverage gave a smile of approval regarding the sweet Chai tea.

Ami, eager that Ryan had asked, attempted to hide her excitement. She realized Ryan was older than she by approximately six or eight years, from her best calculations. She had seen him come and go from the coffee shop for a few years, and had often fantasized about the two of them being together and what it would be like to have Ryan as a respective mate. After she felt that she had paused long enough to make here response not seem over anxious, she spoke.

Ami struggled with her response. "Oh, absolutely. I would. Uhhm. Yeah. I sure would."

Ryan raised his cup of coffee, and turned to face the door. "Interesting. Well, have a great night, and mentally prepare for that, Ami. You never know when the time may come."

As Ryan walked to his car, he considered taking Ami on a date, and what common interests they may have. He considered the possibility of her having no similar sexual interest, and being completely opposed to his desires. As he unlocked his car, he decided there was no real way of determining what Ami's sexual interests were short of actually finding from either asking or attempting.

Ryan placed his beverage into the cup holder and turned on the key to his car. As soon as the dash lights were illuminated, the low tire pressure warning lamp illuminated. Frustrated, Ryan pulled the door handle and opened the door. As he stepped from the car, he looked at the two tires on the driver's side of the car, which were sufficiently inflated.

As he walked around the front bumper, he noticed the right side of the car sagging. As he reached the passenger side of the car, it was immediately apparent that the right front tire was completely flat. After a quick inspection of the tire, he began to become angry, considering the two times the tire had been repaired in the last month. Knowing that the BMW sedan did not have a spare tire, he realized he was nothing short of stranded.

Frustrated and angry, he turned and walked back into the coffee shop.

Ami chuckled as Ryan walked in the front door. "Decide to ask me on that date already?"

Feeling guilty and fractionally selfish, Ryan sighed. "Not yet. Ami, I'm sorry. My car has a flat, and to make a long story short, I'm stranded. One disadvantage of that particular model is that it has no spare tire. There is nowhere at eleven o'clock at night that I will find a tire, and I will need to get a ride home. At what time do you close?"

"We close in three minutes. I'll be here for about forty five minutes after that, cleaning up. I could...let me think." Ami paused and raised her hand to her mouth. "My brother has this patrol. I could see what he's doing. His shift ends at eleven. That's in just a minute."

"The police officer?" Ryan said in a reluctant tone.

Ami pulled her phone from her pocket. "Yeah, but he's cool. He's really nice. If he's not busy, he could give you a ride, or you could wait for me, either way. Let me see if he's even available."

Ryan placed his hands on his hips and attempted to hide his frustration as Ami typed into the screen of her phone. He considered the police officer taking him home, and what harm could come from it. As he decided there was no risk to speak of from riding with the officer,

Ami spoke.

Ami grinned. "He just responded. He's a few miles from here. He'll be here in a five or ten minutes. He said he'd gladly give you a ride. He might even have a cool story to tell you on the way home, he always does."

Ryan nodded. "Thank you, I appreciate it."

Ami walked toward the front door. "I hate to, but we're closing. I have to ask you to go outside. I'm really sorry."

Ryan turned toward the door. "Oh, not at all."

Ami pulled the door open and held it as she waited for Ryan. As Ryan walked past her, he smiled.

"Ami, thank you again. Tell him I'm waiting in the white BMW. The one with a flat." He chuckled.

"No problem, you owe me," she said.

Frustrated, Ryan walked to his car. Although he appreciated Ami's brother providing a ride, he felt uneasy about getting in the car with a police officer. As he sat in the car and waited, he turned on the ignition, rolled down the windows, and sipped his now luke-warm beverage.

As he reclined his seat and began to relax, he noticed a shadow out of his left eye. As he turned and gazed out of his vehicle's open window, he was facing the barrel of a large caliber revolver pointed directly at his face.

CHAPTER TWENTY - SIX

REMEMBER ME?

TWENTY - SIX. "You son-of-a-bitch. I'm going to give you what you deserve. Don't move," a familiar female voice demanded.

Ryan slumped in the seat and stared straight ahead.

"You-son-of-a-bitch. You've ruined my life. I can't sleep, I can't eat. I can't do anything. You and your God forsaken game. You sick bastard, you've ruined my life."

Ryan turned to face the voice.

Dana stood outside of his car, approximately six feet away, pointing a large revolver at his face. Her hands shook as she spoke.

"My cancer is malignant. I have three or four weeks to live," she blubbered.

"I have nothing to lose."

The barrel of the pistol shook as she spoke.

"The thought of leaving this earth and not taking you with me is something that I can't imagine."

She inhaled a long slow breath and cocked the hammer back. "The difference, asshole, is I am going to heaven and you are going to hell."

Dana's voice became more elevated as she spoke.

Ryan raised his hands. "Dana, take it easy. We can…"

"Don't you tell me how to take it," she screamed.

Ryan considered what to say. As he sat in the car and watched the barrel of the pistol shake, he wondered what prevented Dana from shooting him already. Assuming she must have things she wanted to say prior to killing him, he decided to attempt to get her to talk.

"Dana, God isn't going to support you on this. You…"

"Shut up. Just shut up. I hate you, you son-of-a-bitch."

Standing a few feet from his car with the pistol leveled at Ryan's head, Dana began to cry.

As she held the pistol in her right hand, she used her left hand to wipe the tears from her eyes. Ryan placed his hands on the steering wheel in hope of Dana becoming more comfortable that he wasn't a threat.

"Freeze. Drop the weapon, ma'am," A male voice from behind the car demanded.

Ryan glanced into the rear view mirror. A police officer stood behind a patrol car, his arms outstretched over the hood, pointing his service weapon toward Dana. Ryan shifted his gaze from the mirror to his open window.

"He. He's a monster," Dana said.

"Ma'am, drop the weapon. There' is nothing worth losing your life over," the officer shouted.

"But he…" Dana pleaded.

"Drop the weapon," the officer demanded; his voice much louder each time he shouted the command.

Out of Ryan's left eye, he saw Dana's body rotate slightly. As soon as her body began to move, he heard the gunshots.

Pop!

Pop!

Dana's body fell beside his car.

Ryan shifted his gaze to the rearview mirror.

"Sir, are you armed?" the officer screamed.

"Armed?" Ryan screamed out the window as he continued to look out the rearview mirror.

The sound of distant sirens increasingly got louder as the seconds passed.

"No. Sir, have you been *harmed*?" the officer screamed.

"Only my pride officer," Ryan shouted out the window.

"Sir, stay in the vehicle," the officer demanded.

Ami ran toward the police car. "Oh my God Ryan, are you okay?"

"Ami, get back in the store," the officer shouted.

"Is he okay?" Ami screamed.

"Yes, he's fine," the officer responded.

"Sir, stay in the vehicle," the officer stated.

"Until you advise me otherwise," Ryan responded.

Ryan sat, relieved that the officer did not provide immediate medical attention to Dana as she lay on the parking lot bleeding. He hoped, more than anything, that she was dead, or at minimum, incapable of speaking. He watched out the rearview mirror as the officer spoke into the microphone of his radio.

As other officers pulled into the parking lot, they discussed Dana still having *control* of the weapon that was in her hand. Although Ryan could not see, apparently, she was still holding the weapon as she lay on the asphalt in a puddle of blood.

After a long discussion, one of the officers approached as another followed, his weapon pointed at Dana's body the entire time. As the officer got within foot's reach, he kicked the weapon from her hand.

"Clear," the officer shouted.

An officer picked the weapon up from the ground.

Immediately, paramedics rushed to Dana's body. Within seconds, it was apparent that Dana was, in fact, dead. Ryan waited as the paramedics loaded her onto a stretcher and into an ambulance. Who he assumed was Ami's brother approached the driver's side of the car, and advised Ryan that he could exit the vehicle's passenger side.

Ryan crawled across the seats of the car, and opened the passenger side door and stepped into the parking lot.

As soon as Ryan exited the car, Ami rushed to him and embraced him in a hug. "I'm so glad you weren't hurt."

"So am I," Ryan responded.

"I'm sorry you had to witness that," Ryan apologized.

Ami released him from her arms.

Ami shrugged, showing almost no expression. "Oh. Well, to tell you the truth, I'm not. Blood and violence turn me on. Call me weird, but it does. Always has."

His eyes widened. "You don't say?"

And his mouth began to form a smile.

CHAPTER TWENTY- SEVEN

NOT AGAIN.

TWENTY - SEVEN. "I like your dress," the cashier said cheerily.

Meghan smiled as she pressed her hands along the fabric that covered her upper thighs. "Thank you, it's…well, I just got it."

She had purchased the dress earlier in the day at the mall, carefully picking out one that was as revealing as possible without appearing to be *slutty*. The young lady that helped her told her she looked *hot*.

Meghan chuckled, knowing Ryan would certainly approve of *hot*.

"That'll be $37.11," the cashier said as the last of the groceries slid past the scanner.

As the young man at the end of the check-out placed the items into plastic bags, Meghan dug through her wallet for exact change. She expected this evening to be another entertaining time with Ryan. They had made plans to spend the night together, and she intended on cooking him a memorable meal, having some wine, and hopefully another night of sex. She smiled as she handed the cashier the money for her groceries.

The young man held the bags up from the counter. "Would you like help out?"

"No, I can carry them, thank you," Meghan responded.

Ryan had stated his need to resolve some financial business and changed their plans for dinner to a much later time. Meghan preferred to eat earlier, but willingly agreed to accept the plans for a late meal. The opportunity to see Ryan excited her greatly. It had been two days since their first sexual encounter, and it was all Meghan could do to not spend every waking moment recalling each instant of their time together. As she walked to the car, Meghan wondered what Ryan may be planning. The not knowing caused her to smile as she made her way across the dark parking lot.

She pressed the button on her key fob, unlocking the vehicle. After she placed the groceries into the rear compartment of her SUV, she turned to close the door. As the door swung closed, she saw a bright flash of light, and felt a sharp pain in her armpit. When she awoke, her hands were bound, her feet were bound, and her mouth was gagged. Her head felt as if it was covered with some form of fabric, and her surrounding was completely dark.

As she blinked her eyes and tried unsuccessfully to see, she felt as if she was in a moving vehicle. She realized as she felt the vehicle begin to drive away that contrary to when Ryan captured her, she now felt no excitement or state of arousal regarding her abduction. As she sensed the vehicle turning a corner, she began to develop a deep fear. Fear of losing her daughter, of losing whatever she may have with Ryan, and fear of losing her life began to race through her mind.

She attempted to straighten her legs, and as she did, she felt a strain on her shoulders. As she tried again, she determined that her feet and her hands were bound together - her hands behind her back. Incapable of screaming, and her head covered in some form of fabric, she began to cry.

Consumed with her feeling of fear, and wondering why her conscious thoughts differed from when she was abducted by Ryan,

Meghan attempted to force herself to desire what *was* happening to *be* happening. Try as she might, she continued to cry uncontrollably. Frantically, she kicked her legs, each time pulling a tremendous strain on her shoulders.

As she felt the car turn another corner, Meghan began to consider that her options regarding escape were very limited. Attempts to convince herself to comply with any and all wishes by her captor began to make her feel queasy. Thoughts of being raped, forced to perform sexual acts, or any other form of sexual contact began to make her stomach convulse.

Struggling with potential scenarios of what may happen if and when she was removed from her confinement of the vehicle, being compliant continued to enter her mind. Considering being as cooperative as possible became her only viable option, with an escape as soon as she was able. As she planned a way of attempting to overcome her captor, she felt the car come to a stop.

A car door opening and closing.

The trunk opening.

A sharp pain in her side.

Darkness.

When Meghan regained consciousness, she was lying on a cold concrete floor. Although her mouth was no longer gagged, she was still bound. As she heard footsteps across the floor in front of her, she pulled against the restraints that bound her hands. There was minimal slack in what was used to bind her, and her feeble attempts only provided strain on her shoulders as she attempted to pull upward with her hands.

"Please, I'll do anything if you release me," Meghan begged softly as she lay on the cold floor.

She heard her captor exhale, and felt a hand on her cheek. The fingers pressed against the skin of her face harshly and slipped by her lips. As they began to work their way into her mouth, she lightly attempted to close it. The fingers were immediately withdrawn.

Whack!

She felt a hand strike her face with tremendous force. Wanting to make this encounter as painless as possible, as the tears began to run from her eyes, she opened her mouth and rolled onto her back. As she lay on her back, she felt fingers in her hair and an immediate tremendous strain on the top of her scalp. She was being picked up by her hair.

"Oh my God. No, no," she cried as she attempted to stand.

Her hands being bound to her legs didn't allow her much free movement, making standing from her position on the floor almost impossible without assistance. She felt as if her hair was being pulled from her head. As she kicked her legs and attempted to stand, she felt herself being lifted from the floor. Now in a semi-crouched position on her knees, the tears streamed from her eyes and soaked her blindfold.

"Please, anything. I'll do anything," she sobbed.

Again, Meghan felt the hand against her face. She opened her mouth. The fingers pushed past her lips, along her tongue, and deep into her throat. As her throat convulsed and she gagged, her eyes began to water even more. Rapidly, the fingers worked in and out of her mouth, causing her to gag repeatedly. As she fought to breathe, the fingers slid in and out of her mouth until she felt saliva dripping from her chin.

As the hand was removed from her mouth, she attempted to catch her breath, gasping to fill her lungs with air. A hand pressed against each cheek, holding her head stable. As she felt the two thumbs press hard against her chin, forcing her jaw to open wide, she feared what was next.

The hands released her face and pushed along her neck and into the top of her dress. As she felt them slide into her bra, she shuddered. Groping and squeezing her breasts, the fingers kneaded her flesh harshly. She felt her nipples being pinched hard, and bit her bottom lip to prevent from screaming.

The fingers pinched her nipples until she became numb to the pain. As she felt the hands slide from her bra, she sighed and released the pressure from her bottom lip. She heard a sharp *click*, felt pressure against her wrists, and then relief from being bound. A hand pressed between her calf muscles, and she felt pressure against the restraints on her ankles. Immediately, she felt relief from her leg bindings.

A hand slid under her armpit and assisted her in standing. Her knees burning from the concrete floor, she stood. As she was being led across the floor, she walked hesitantly, fearing what she may encounter. Her captor's hand pressed against her upper back, forcing her to bend over. As she bent at the waist, she held her hands in front of her to stabilize herself from falling. With her arms extended, she felt a cold flat surface, and pressed her hands against it.

She felt pressure against the back of her head, and the same sharp *click* she heard earlier. As the pressure against her eyes from the blindfold was relieved, she opened her eyes. The bright light was blinding at first, causing her to blink, allowing her eyes to adjust.

As her eyes adjusted to the light, she focused what stood before her. And she trembled.

CHAPTER TWENTY - EIGHT

I LOVE IT WHEN A PLAN COMES TOGETHER.

TWENTY - EIGHT. Meghan blinked her eyes in disbelief as she faced three large Asian men wearing very expensive looking suits. The room in which she was now standing became immediately familiar.

Meghan was standing in the room she and the other three girls were held captive in. She blinked her eyes and turned to see Ryan standing behind her, smiling. As her mind began to process what was happening, she instantly felt relief, followed by a sinking fear.

"Ryan, oh my God. What is going on?" she gasped.

Ryan hugged her for a moment, and broke the embrace as he spoke. "You like it rough and kinky. Here we are. This is what I want."

He motioned toward the Asian men.

Meghan glanced toward the Asian men, who stood statue still, staring straight ahead. They were all very large; approximately six foot tall and two hundred pounds by her best estimate. They appeared to be a mirror image of each other in appearance, dress, and physique. She turned from the men and faced Ryan.

"I'm really confused," Meghan whispered.

"I'll explain it to you. You like excitement and BDSM, so I thought I'd shock you. You're going to do what I say, and pretty soon this will be over. I need you to do as I tell you- willingly. It's important that you do it willingly and don't fight it. Do you understand?" Ryan asked softly.

Meghan blinked her eyes. "Okay. Okay, I guess, yeah."

Consumed with wonder, Meghan began to feel relief that Ryan had some form of plan, and that he decided to cut her bindings and remove her blindfold. As the reality of where they were began to sink in, Meghan took a shallow breath and exhaled.

"Can we go somewhere else? This room. Well, it creeps me out, Ryan. Can we go somewhere else?" Meghan pleaded.

"That's enough talking. I need you to get on your knees and suck my cock, Meghan. Do it now," Ryan said sternly as he unzipped his slacks.

As Ryan reached into his pants and pulled out his cock, Meghan quickly realized he was serious. A small degree of excitement was followed with a larger feeling of embarrassment, and then shame. As she looked at Ryan with confusion on her face, he placed his hands on her shoulders. As he pushed her to her knees, she began to feel uneasy.

"Ryan, this is weird, I…" Meghan tried to reason.

"Meghan, I need you to suck my cock while these guys watch. This is only the beginning, but this will all be over before you know it, okay?" Ryan said in a stern tone.

As Ryan began to stroke his cock, Meghan glanced at the Asian men in suits, still standing erect and expressionless against the bench along the wall. The thought of them watching her suck Ryan's cock began to excite her. As she shifted her gaze to Ryan, she saw his cock becoming hard in his hand.

"Open," Ryan whispered as he stepped toward her.

Meghan closed her eyes and opened her mouth. As he felt Ryan's cock enter her mouth, she pressed against the bottom of the shaft with her tongue. For some reason, desperately, she wanted not only Ryan to be pleased with her, but for the men watching to be impressed with her abilities.

As Ryan's length slid in and out of her mouth, she remembered what Ryan had said in her home regarding her hands. She opened her eyes and placed her hands on her thighs as she eagerly allowed him to fuck her throat. The sound of Ryan's cock pounding against her throat, her gagging, and coughing echoed through the concrete room. As Ryan moaned, Meghan began to feel herself become extremely aroused. She closed her eyes as she felt her pussy become soaked.

The pressure of his hands on her neck startled her and she opened her eyes. As Ryan continued to pound himself in and out of her throat, he pulled upward against her neck with his hands, lifting her weight from the floor.

"Stand," Ryan demanded.

Ryan's stiffness flopped from her mouth as she straightened her legs and began to stand.

"Remove your dress," Ryan whispered.

Meghan, now immune to what else was surrounding her, quickly struggled with pulling her dress over her shoulders. As she tossed it on the bench beside her, Ryan nodded toward her and pointed to her panties. She pressed her thumbs against her hips, and pushed her panties down her thighs and over her knees. As she lifted her feet from the floor, Ryan reached behind her and unclasped her bra. Her clothes now on a pile on the bench, Ryan stood before her in slacks, a white t-shirt, and dress shoes.

"Meghan, the man on the left. You're going to suck his cock until he fills your mouth with cum. While you're sucking his cock, I'm going to be fucking you from behind. We will work from left to right, and when you've finished, it will all be over," Ryan whispered.

Meghan turned to face the men who still stood against the bench along the wall. Something about knowing Ryan's will, his desire, and his expectations of her made Meghan feel as if she was pleasing him by doing as he asked. Knowing the overall plan, Ryan's intent, and that there was a goal began to excite Meghan. Sucking all of the men's cocks to completion, however, was somewhat overwhelming.

As she stepped toward the man on the left, he unzipped his pants and removed his rather large dick. Without speaking, he placed his hands on his hips. Meghan glanced at Ryan. An affirmative nod was all she needed. She positioned herself in front of the man, bent at the waist, placed her hands on her knees, and wrapped her lips around the man's cock.

She eagerly sucked the stranger's dick, hoping for him to cum as quickly as possible. She felt Ryan's thickness pressing against her soaking wet pussy. As he began to penetrate her deeply, she immediately reached climax. As she did, she groaned against the thick shaft that filled her mouth.

Rhythmically, Ryan's swollen shaft slid in and out of her pussy as she sucked the stranger no differently that she had sucked Ryan. Forcefully. She opened her eyes and looked up toward his face making note that he was staring straight ahead expressionless. She closed her eyes and continued to suck and gag on his cock – pounding it into the back of her throat with each stroke.

Thinking of sucking all of the men to completion changed from overwhelming to exciting. As Meghan felt her pussy begin to contract again, she moaned. As she moaned, she felt the head swell in her throat.

Knowing he was reaching climax, she eagerly worked her mouth up and down the shaft.

As his cock began to pulse, Meghan felt his cum enter her throat. She pressed her mouth against the base of the shaft, allowing his cum into her throat. As the man finished ejaculating, he pulled his swollen shaft from her mouth and nodded his head.

Meghan glanced to the man on her right as he unzipped his zipper and pulled his similarly shaped and sized penis from his pants. As she started to shuffle her way to the right, the man directly in front of her moved aside, and the man in the middle stepped in front of her.

She leaned forward and wrapped her lips around the tip of his dick, and inhaled through her nose. She closed her eyes and began working her mouth up and down the shaft, lubricating it well. She decided to try a different technique, and see if she could cause him to cum more quickly. As Ryan's cock began to work its way in and out of her pussy, she started to aggressively suck the man's cock as fast as she could.

As she gagged and slobbered all over the man's shaft, Ryan pummeled her pussy. The faster she sucked, the faster Ryan fucked her pussy. Proud of her determination, Meghan sucked the man's dick as if it was her only desire. Ryan's hands squeezed her hips firmly as he forced himself deeper and deeper with each stroke. As her entire body began to tingle, she pressed her hands against her knees and squeezed. If she didn't collapse from this orgasm, she felt it would be a miracle. As her body tingled from her nipples to her clit, she groaned in ecstasy.

With her groans came the immediate reward of the warm cum against her tongue. As soon as she felt him cum, she buried her mouth on the shaft, allowing his cum deep in her throat. As her eyes rolled from the earth shattering orgasm, the second man pulled himself from her mouth.

"One…more," Ryan said breathlessly. "And then…then it…it's over."

Surprised at her elevated arousal, Meghan opened her eyes and stared at the wall as the man stepped aside and the third man moved in front of her. With a strange level of an almost disappointment that this was going to end, she took a shallow breath and smiled. As the man unzipped his zipper and pulled his cock from his pants, Meghan pressed her hands against her now very sore knees.

"I almost collapsed from that orgasm, it was intense," she said over her shoulder.

"I'm sure it was. It's almost over," Ryan assured her.

"I almost don't want it to end," Meghan admitted.

Ryan inhaled a deep breath. "Neither do I, Meghan."

Meghan grinned.

"Neither do I," he repeated.

"Last one," Meghan smiled as she wrapped her lips around the swollen shaft.

Deciding to attempt to repeat the process, Meghan sucked as eagerly as she could. Almost immediately, she felt the man's girth begin to swell in her mouth. Ryan's hands slid to her breasts. As he forcefully pounded himself in and out of her soaking wet pussy, he began to squeeze her breasts in his hands and pull downward on her nipples. A feeling of shock traveled through her body from her nipples to her clit.

Simultaneously, as Meghan started to climax, she felt Ryan's cock begin to swell inside of her. As it swelled against the inner walls of her vaginal canal, she reached a level of climax that shook her legs. As Ryan groaned, she buried her mouth onto the third man's shaft. Her eyes rolled as she felt the pulsation in her mouth and his cum squirt down her throat.

As she groaned in ecstasy, she felt Ryan's cum shoot against her cervix.

A feeling of elation filled her as Ryan groaned. Knowing that he was pleased with her, and that she had completed the task that he had placed in front of her caused her tremendous satisfaction. The thought of Ryan cumming inside of her filled Meghan with a level of pleasure that she had not felt for years. As the man's dick fell from her mouth, Ryan slid from inside of her.

She pressed her hands against her knees and stood.

Meghan stood and turned to face Ryan. "Oh my God. My legs are done. God that was exhausting."

She reached over Ryan's shoulders and embraced him, exhausted. As she hugged him, she felt grateful that she had met him, regardless of the circumstances surrounding their having met. He was, by all accounts, exactly what she always wanted and felt that she needed. She leaned away from his shoulder and looked up into his eyes.

"That last orgasm. God, I thought it was going to kill me," Meghan sighed.

Ryan's mouth twisted into a smirk. "Fuck it, you're going to die anyway."

As Meghan scrunched her brow, her mind filled with confusion.

She heard a familiar *click*. Quickly, Ryan's arm rose to her shoulder level, and she felt a scratch against her neck. As she raised her hands to rub the itch on her neck, Ryan stepped back and smiled. Meghan smiled in return as her fingers fumbled along the base of her neck. The smile quickly turned to a frown, followed by a look of despair.

As wet warmth covered her hands and neck.

As Meghan pulled her hands from her neck and looked at her fingers, she collapsed into a puddle of blood that had dripped from her breasts and elbows. As she lay on the floor, dying in a pool of her own blood, Ryan stepped over her body. She attempted to rotate her head and see where he was going, but was incapable of moving. As she pressed her hands to her neck, and gasped her final living breaths, she blinked her eyes in wonder.

And the last thing she heard was another familiar sound.

The door closed.

And the door lock mechanism clicked.

CHAPTER TWENTY - NINE

GRADUATION DAY.

TWENTY- NINE. The announcement echoed throughout the auditorium. *"Ladies and gentlemen, mothers and fathers, brothers and sisters, friends and associates, I present to you the graduating class of 2012."*

As the children hugged their respective parents, friends, and family members, Ryan watched the girl work her way through the crowd. As she approached the rear of the auditorium, he walked toward the exit closest to him, paying close attention to the movements of the girl through the overfilled auditorium. Dressed in her graduation gown and holding her cap, she closely resembled every other girl in the crowd.

Ryan watched as the girl walked to the exit, pressed her hands against the door, hesitated, and looked back into the auditorium. After a moment's wait, she turned to face the door again. As she pushed the door open on the other side of the auditorium, Ryan opened the door at the opposite end and walked outside, clutching the gym bag in his hand as he attempted to follow her across the courtyard unnoticed.

Staying approximately one hundred feet behind the girl as she walked toward the parking lot, Ryan watched as she approached a twenty year old Honda Prelude and started to unlock the door. As she fumbled to insert the key in door's lock cylinder, she glanced attentively around the parking lot.

Ryan increased his pace as she opened the door. Nervously, he scanned the parking lot for witnesses. Seeing no one within eye shot, he increased his walking speed to an almost jog toward the car as the girl rolled down the window. As he stepped to the driver's door of the car, the girl was unsuccessfully attempting to start the car.

"You little piece of shit, start. Come on. *Start*," the girl pleaded as she cranked the engine of the car over.

As the engine cranked, the battery became weaker, turning the engine slower and slower.

Softly Ryan spoke, trying not to startle the girl. "Excuse me, are you having problems?"

The girl quickly turned to face Ryan, startled by his voice. As she looked out of the vehicle's window and up into Ryan's eyes, he immediately noticed the similarities between her and her mother. As she made eye contact, she stopped trying to start the car.

She shrugged. "Sometimes it doesn't want to go. It'll start in a minute."

Ryan raised the gym bag, feeling considerably more nervous than he expected. "Well. I have something for you."

The girl's eyes fell to Ryan's shoes, and then rose to his face. "Excuse me? You don't know me. Are you a cop?"

"No. I am not a police officer."

Ryan took a step away from the car, attempting to make the girl more comfortable with his presence. "Are you Jessica Rodriguez?"

"Who wants to know? Is this about my mother?"

Ryan fumbled with his choice of words. "Well, yes. In a sense, I suppose."

The girl opened the door and stepped out of her car, now standing between Ryan and her car.

Ryan extended his arm, holding the gym bag in his hand. "I'll do my best to explain. I'm quite wealthy. I learned of your mother's disappearance through a friend of a friend. I know that you're an only child, and you'll be eighteen soon. I know if your mother doesn't resurface, you'll have a difficult life."

The girl looked down at the gym bag.

Ryan swallowed a lump in his throat as he held the bag at arm's length. "Here, take this. It's for you."

She motioned toward the bag. "So, yeah. I'm Jessica. What is it?"

Ryan sighed and placed the bag on the ground between them. "It's a graduation gift."

Jessica smiled and reached for the bag. Startled by the weight as she attempted to lift it, she raised her eyebrows in wonder.

"Let me explain, please." Ryan crossed his arms and inhaled a slow breath, still feeling rather uncomfortable speaking to Jessica. "It's money. Actually, it's a *lot* of money. You're going to need to…"

"Why you wanna give me money? You don't know me."

Ryan uncrossed his arms and pushed his hands into his front pockets. "Just look at it as a graduation gift. You'll need to be careful how you spend it, because spending large amounts of cash is frowned upon. But that should get you by for some time. Maybe. if you're wise, a lifetime."

Jessica bent over and unzipped the bag. She peered inside. Shocked, she glanced up at Ryan, and then into the bag again. Carefully, she reached into the bag and shuffled the money around, looking through the banded bundles of fifty dollar bills in wonder.

She looked at Ryan and widened her eyes.

Ryan rocked back and forth on the balls of his feet. "It's seven hundred thousand dollars, a graduation gift from me to you. Just in case you end up alone through all of this."

She picked the bag up and pulled it close to her body, clutching it in both arms. "You're serious. You're giving this to me?"

Ryan smiled an awkward smile, feeling fairly certain that the girl was going to accept the money as a gift. "I am an only child. I know what it's like to be an only child. I am fortunate to have my parents and can't imagine trying to go about living life alone. When I learned of the disappearance of your mother, I decided I wanted to do this for you, just in case she doesn't come home."

"I don't even know what to say," she said, her voiced filled with emotion.

Ryan shrugged. "Say nothing."

Jessica turned and faced her car as she clutched the bag.

"You need a ride somewhere?" Ryan asked.

"Well," Jessica said over her shoulder.

Ryan motioned across the parking lot toward his car. "It's probably not a good idea to get stranded with that amount of cash. I'm parked right over there."

"The white car?"

Ryan nodded. "I can give you a ride to the dealership out on east Kellogg. I know the manager. He'll maybe let you pay cash for an inexpensive car – something that will start when you want it to."

She grinned. "Well, I suppose."

"You can come back and get your belongings later if you prefer," Ryan offered.

Jessica struggled with the weight of the bag. "Well, this is weird. I don't know what to…"

Ryan reached toward the bag. "Here, let me carry it for you,"

Jessica hefted the bag up and clutched it tight against her body. "No, I got it."

"Yeah, you can give me a ride. You really think I can buy a car?" she asked.

Ryan felt an odd sense of satisfaction as they began to walk toward his car. "I'm sure of it."

Clutching the bag against her chest, Jessica walked beside Ryan, smiling a little more with each step.

"So tell me about your mother," Ryan said.

"Well, her name is Elena…"

As Jessica spoke, Ryan listened intently. The value that the girl placed on her mother made Ryan uneasy and jealous. Elena, to Jessica, was both her best friend and her mother – something Ryan never had in a parent. As they reached the car, Ryan pressed the button on his key fob and unlocked the doors.

As Ryan reached for the door handle, he took a slow breath and did something he had not done since his childhood.

The little fat boy inside of him prayed to God.

For Jessica's well-being.

CHAPTER THIRTY

CHECK PLEASE.

THIRTY. Ami raised her hands to her face and pressed her fingers against her cheeks. "I don't know, it just always has. Ever since I was a kid and my dad took us deer hunting."

"The smell of gunpowder and blood?" Ryan asked, making sure of her statement.

Ami nodded. "Yeah. I'm sorry if it creeps you out. But it's just a huge turn on."

Ryan chuckled. "No, I suppose not. I'm not concerned."

Ami smiled as she raised her glass of wine to her mouth. "It just seems weird being with you away from the coffee shop. You know, like actually sitting and talking to you. The good kind of weird."

"The good kind of weird." Ryan laughed as he placed his index finger against his upper lip and admired Ami's dress.

The plunging neckline revealed a considerable portion of Ami's breasts, but was elegant enough to not make her appear *cheap* in any way. Her careful choice of complimentary jewelry was very tasteful as were her conservative three inch heels. All things considered, Ryan believed Ami, as she sat before him, to be the most attractive woman he had ever seen.

Ryan tapped his finger on his lip nervously. "Your dress is stunning,

Ami. What a great choice."

Ami leaned toward Ryan, resting her forearms on the table and cupped her hands together. As she looked up into Ryan's eyes, her breasts heaved as she breathed. Ryan attempted not to stare, feeling his level of already heightened arousal begin to rise even more. As he felt his cock begin to become stiff, he pressed the heel of his palm against his erection and smiled.

"If you want the truth, I have a spending problem." Ami slurred her speech as she pronounced *spending*.

"Oh really?" Ryan asked, hoping to keep Ami in this position for as long as possible.

Ami raised her left hand to her face and brushed her hair behind her ear. As she pulled her hand away from her face, she covered her mouth lightly and giggled. Tilting her head to the right, she tried to reveal her tattoo to Ryan's watchful eyes. She noticed his eyes alternating glances between her eyes and her breasts, and intending on leaning over the table as long as she could possibly do so.

"I think I've had too much wine," Ami said, knowing very well that she hadn't.

She raised one eyebrow and waited for Ryan to respond.

"Define too much," Ryan responded.

"Well. I've reached the point of brutal honesty. You know the two most honest people on the planet?" Ami asked.

Ryan smiled as he continued to admire Ami's natural beauty. "Who's that?"

"Kids and drunks," Ami whispered.

"You don't say," Ryan said as he leaned a few inches closer.

Ami giggled. "I just said."

Ami inhaled a long deep breath and held it as long as she could, exhaling slowly. She had imagined what Ryan would be like in person for some time now, and was quite pleased with his intriguing nature, handsome looks, and solid muscular build. Ami lowered her chin to almost touch the table, and curled her index finger, motioning for Ryan to come closer.

"I steal stuff," Ami whispered as Ryan's face moved within a foot of hers.

"Oh really? Why?" Ryan smiled as he asked the question.

Ami turned to her head in either direction, verifying that there was no one within earshot. Her face felt flush from her last glass of wine. Three was certainly more than she generally drank, but the initial thought of Ryan made her nervous, and she intended to just have enough to loosen up. At his insistence, she had ordered the third. She focused on Ryan and raised her palms, resting them against her cheeks.

"It's exciting and I like expensive stuff. Something about stealing makes me feel like a criminal, and I just love it. I know it's childish and I should stop, but it's really a rush to do it," she said.

"Interesting," Ryan said flatly.

"You're interesting," Ami snapped back.

"You think so," Ryan asked.

"Know so," Ami responded before Ryan had actually finished speaking.

Ryan grinned. "Well, I'm *not* drunk, but I suspect I owe it to you to be brutally honest with you."

Ami looked into Ryan's eyes and blinked exaggeratedly. "Shoot."

"Well, I'm all but sick of living here, and I'm ready to get out of this place. As I am sure you can tell that I am, and I have been attracted to you for some time. I just don't see myself staying here." Ryan paused and waited for Ami to respond.

Ami glanced at her half full glass of wine and shifted her eyes to Ryan again. Without looking, she reached over and slid the glass in front of her face. With her chin still resting in her right hand, and maintaining focus on Ryan, she tipped the glass to her lips and finished the wine.

"I hate this god forsaken city," Ami said through her teeth.

"But you're in college, you need to finish," Ryan said, hoping for a response that he didn't expect.

Ami turned, looked at her empty glass, and rolled her eyes. "I don't *need* to finish. I need entertained."

"Well, along those lines, I have another subject I guess we should discuss." Ryan sat back in his chair and studied Ami's face.

The night, as far as Ryan was concerned, had gone remarkably well. Although this was their first date, he felt an immediate connection to Ami. He had desired her for years, and while he felt that previous desire *could* have come into play, he believed his current attraction was solely based on what he learned of her from this dinner date. She, by all standards, was exactly what he desired, hoped for, and felt that he needed.

Wondering about his ability to actually have any form of long-term relationship, and continue to feed his potential desire for what he believed to borderline psychotic behavior, he stared at Ami and smiled.

"It's a sexual statement," Ryan said softly.

Ami sighed heavily. "Finally."

Ryan smiled at Ami's response. Although he doubted it, if Ami's sexual desires were comparable to what his expectations of his own were, he felt he may be able to make something work. With no expectation,

238

and a minimal amount of hope, he decided to be brutally honest. After all, her drunken state would certainly soften her response somewhat if she was offended.

"Well, sexually." Embarrassed, Ryan stumbled with his words. He inhaled a breath through his nose, exhaled, and continued. "Sexually speaking, my wants, needs, and desires borderline criminal behavior."

Ami batted her eyelashes and stared at Ryan. "Thank God."

He grinned. "I mean, you have no idea."

"Thank God," Ami responded.

"They're incomprehensible," Ryan whispered.

Ami turned, looked at her empty glass again, faced Ryan, and rolled her eyes. "Enlighten me. Give me a *for instance*. A really fucking good one."

Ryan sat back in his chair and thought. Quite shocked at Ami's lack of concern regarding his potential sexual desires, he became excited about the possibility of her truly being the woman of his dreams. In a perfect world, if she were a sexual deviant, a murderer, and obsessed with money, he felt that they just might make it. As he chuckled to himself, he realized that she could potentially meet two out of three, considering her problem with stealing expensive articles of clothing.

Ryan leaned toward the center of the table and rested his hands on his chin. He inhaled a short breath through his mouth and exhaled. His face a matter of inches from Ami's, he could feel her sweet breath against his lips.

"I tied a woman to a bed once," Ryan lied. "And I fucked her face until she was almost unconscious. Then I untied her, turned her over and fucked her from behind until she couldn't stand."

Ami batted her eyelashes and stared into Ryan's eyes. "After that, did you do anything exciting?"

"That's only the beginning," Ryan assured her, again lying.

Ami rolled her eyes. "Thank God. Because that sounded borderline vanilla to me."

Trying to hide his excitement, Ryan chuckled lightly.

"You know…" Ami inhaled, pursed her lips, and blew her cheeks out as she exhaled. She gazed into Ryan's eyes. "You know how you meet someone, and you just *know*. Like you know that person is *the* person?"

He smiled. "I suppose, why?"

Ami nodded. "Because I think you're *that* person."

He tilted his head and raised his palms in wonder. "You really think so?"

"I think *this*. I would follow you to the fiery depths of hell."

"To hell?" Ryan asked.

"To fucking hell," Ami responded.

He grinned. "To hell we're headed."

She shook her head. "Not quick enough."

"You ready?" he asked.

She cocked an eyebrow. "To follow you?"

He nodded.

"To hell?" she asked.

Ryan nodded once sharply. "To fucking hell."

Ami raised her right hand over her head and locked her elbow. With her eyes locked on his, she cocked her head toward the aisle of the restaurant.

"Check please," she shouted.

EPILOGUE

Even though the sun had been down for hours, the temperature was almost too much to bear. The Arizona summers often had temperatures at night in excess of a hundred degrees until long after sundown.

"It's so fucking hot. I can't believe you want the top off of this thing," Ryan laughed.

"It's a Jeep. It shouldn't even *have* a top. You should take that little fabric fucker and toss it in the dumpster," Ami responded.

She glanced toward the gas pumps and quickly shifted her eyes toward Ryan.

"Well?" Ryan asked.

"You can either unzip 'em or I will. Jesus, act like we haven't done this before," she said.

Ryan sighed. "Every time."

"Yeah, every time we do *this*, we fuck *first*. Just in case. I can't take any chances," she responded.

As soon as Ryan unzipped his pants, Ami leaned over the console of the Jeep and began sucking his cock. Her lips worked up and down the thick shaft as it became fully erect in her mouth. As she sucked and slobbered, she cupped Ryan's balls in her hand. Ryan began to moan as Ami groaned in pleasure.

He chuckled and pulled away. Her sucking was much different than Meghan's. With Ami, he wasn't able to last longer than a few seconds

241

without reaching climax.

"I can't take it anymore," he said.

She pulled her mouth from his saliva covered shaft. "Pussy."

He shrugged.

"Move your arm," Ami demanded.

She raised her leg over the console.

He furrowed his brow. "You're going to *face* me?"

He turned and looked out each side of the Jeep and into the empty parking lot.

She shook her head as she climbed into his lap. "It's midnight in the middle of fuckwater Arizona – what are you afraid of? I want you to bite my titties while I ride your cock. Jesus. Can a girl get *any* satisfaction?"

With her dress over her waist and her panties on the floor of the Jeep, she nodded toward his twitching shaft. "Well, pull down your shorts."

She hovered over Ryan's waist, one hand on the console and one on the Jeeps half-door.

As Ryan pushed his cargo shorts to his knees, Ami lowered herself onto his lap. Carefully, as she positioned herself between Ryan and the steering wheel, she reached between Ryan and the jeeps door, pulling the lever to recline the seat. As the seat reclined, she raised her dress to her torso.

"Fuck the shit out of me," Ami growled.

Ryan reached between his legs and guided his stiff cock into Ami's wetness. She gasped at the feeling of him penetrating her slightly. As she lowered herself onto the full length of his swollen shaft, she groaned.

With his cock deep within her, she closed her eyes out of sheer pleasure.

Ryan reached behind her back and placed his hands on top of her shoulders. Pressing his feet to the floorboard of the Jeep, he began to raise and lower his hips slowly.

She opened her eyes wide. "No, fuck me like it's going to be the last time. Each time before we do it."

He sighed.

"Now fuck me," Ami demanded.

Ami began to moan loudly as Ryan increased his speed. The sound of his thighs slapping against her ass and the back side of her legs echoed off of the concrete wall of the gas station. Pulling down on her shoulders, and forcing himself deep inside of her, Ryan began to growl.

"Fuck yes. Growl. God that makes me want to cum. Growl," Ami pleaded as she opened her eyes momentarily.

As Ryan continued to pound himself deeply into Ami's pussy, she reached up and pulled the top of her dress down, revealing her breasts. Ryan's continuous thrusts against her caused them to bounce with each stroke. Grasping her boobs in each of her hands, Ami began to pinch her nipples in between her index fingers and her thumbs.

Her breasts slick from the hot Arizona air, her level of arousal, and the thought of their upcoming adventure, she continued to squeeze them and pinch her nipples to the point of tremendous pain.

"Talk shit while you fuck me baby, or I'm gonna forget you're in there," she said.

"You like that fat cock inside of your tight little pussy, you little whore?"

"Oh hell yes I do," Ami shouted back.

"Squeeze those big titties for me, you cum slut. Pinch those nipples," Ryan demanded.

She pinched her nipples between her fingers and pulled against them sharply. "Yes, Sir. Whatever you say."

"I love filling your little bitty pussy with my huge cock," Ryan bellowed as he pounded deeper and deeper into Ami's soaking wet pussy.

"You're a good little slut."

"Thank you, Sir."

He reached between her thighs and pushed his index finger into her ass.

"Oh God," she wailed.

"You like it in that tight little ass, don't you?"

"Oh God, yes."

"Because you're a…"

"I'm a fucking whore. A slut," she bellowed. "A cum slut."

Ami bounced up and down from the force of Ryan fucking her, her boobs bouncing as her body raised and lowered on his thighs. With her eyes closed, she bit her bottom lip and grunted as she continued to pull on her nipples repeatedly.

"Fuck yes, I'm about there. Fuck me. Oh God. Fuck me. Fuck me. Fuck me. Harder. Harder. Oh God yes. You fucking animal. Fuck me," Ami screamed.

The words echoed throughout the open parking lot.

"I want you to cum all over me. Do you understand me, you little whore?" Ryan mumbled as Ami bounced on his thighs.

"Bite my titties," Ami screamed as she reached over Ryan's shoulder sand grabbed his head.

Pulling his head into her chest, Ami screamed as Ryan began to bite her nipples and growl. His mouth alternating from one to the other, Ryan bit her nipples and pulled against her flesh with his teeth, stretching her breasts outward as he did so. As he continued to bite her breasts, he released her shoulders and wrapped his hands around her neck. His grip tightened with each stroke of his cock into her now soaking wet pussy.

"Oh God yes. Choke me. Choke…"

Ryan's grasp of her neck prevented her from continuing to speak.

With his free hand he slapped her face.

And again, he slapped her.

And again.

He leaned forward and bit her nipples as he buried himself deep into her.

Ami opened her eyes and closed them repeatedly as she looked down and watched Ryan bite her nipples. The large post mounted lamp illuminated her face enough that Ryan could see her eyes roll back as he forced himself even deeper into her pussy.

Ryan's grasp of her neck prevented her from speaking any further. As he choked her tightly, his cock began to swell inside of her. Each upward thrust of his hips caused Ami to groan and grunt. As her eyes bulged and stared straight ahead, he felt himself reach climax.

He released her neck. She coughed and gasped for air.

As Ryan exhaled a loud moan, Ami's vagina clamped down on the shaft of his cock. Gasping for breath, she opened her eyes wide and screamed. As she shouted, the head of Ryan's dick pulsed, filling Ami with his warm cum.

"Holy fuck. Now that's an orgasm. Jesus fucking Christ. Don't you dare move," Ami shouted as she sat still on Ryan's lap.

Ryan wiggled his hips.

She swung her right hand quickly and with great precision.

Whack!

"I said don't move. Don't make me slap your pretty face again," Ami barked.

"You bitch. What did I tell you about slapping me?" Ryan growled as he wiped his hand across his face.

"*Sexy* bitch. And what did I tell you about moving?" Ami asked.

"Fair enough," Ryan said as he wiggled his lower jaw. "Sexy bitch."

"Okay. You about ready?" Ami asked.

Ryan nodded.

Ami rose up from Ryan's lap and slid over the console to the passenger seat. As soon as she sat down, she leaned over the console and wrapped her lips around Ryan's cock, licking it clean of all of the juices from their haphazard parking lot sex.

Ami laughed as she pointed to Ryan's shorts that rested mid-thigh. "Okay, I cleaned up my mess, pull 'em up."

As Ryan pulled up his shorts, Ami raised the strap of her purse over her shoulder and opened the door. She stepped out into the parking lot and surveyed the area for onlookers.

Ryan opened his door and hesitated before he got out of the Jeep.

"Same as last time?" Ryan asked.

Ami stepped around the rear of the Jeep. "Yeah, I mean. Well, yeah."

Ryan grinned and adjusted his shorts. "I love you, baby."

She leaned forward and kissed him on the lips. "I love *you*."

The taste of his own cum on his tongue caused him to grin beneath the kiss.

"To the depths of hell," Ami whispered as she broke the kiss.

"To the depths of hell," Ryan repeated.

Ami away. "Well, here we go."

As they walked toward the front door, they held hands and smiled.

As Ryan opened the door for Ami to enter, she quickly scanned the store for cameras, seeing none. She rolled her eyes and shook her head sharply as she stepped through the threshold of the door, signifying there were no visible cameras.

Once in the store, Ami followed Ryan toward the refrigerated beverage cooler. As he walked in front of the cooler and studied the reflection in the glass, Ami reached both hands into her purse and removed two guns. Ryan raised his index finger, indicating there was only one employee.

As she handed Ryan one of the guns, she winked.

"To the depths of hell," Ryan whispered.

Ami turned to face the cash register. Hiding the pistol beside her leg, she stepped down the aisle, whistling as she walked.

As she walked within a few feet of the cashier, the man behind the counter looked up and grinned.

She raised the pistol level with the man's face. "Alright you sad motherfucker. Today's the day you hoped would never come. No sudden movements or it's gonna get as messy as a shit sandwich."

The man thrust his hands into the air. "No troubles, please."

As Ami stood before the register, Ryan faced the front door, hiding safe behind the cover of the display of chips and crackers.

Ami glanced over her shoulder.

"Clear," Ryan shouted across the store, assuring Ami there were still no patrons approaching.

Ami held the pistol rock-steady in front of the man's face. She nodded her head toward the register and chuckled as she read the man's nametag. "Empty the register, *Mo*. Is that short for Mohammed?"

As she held the barrel of the pistol inches from his forehead, he reached toward the register.

Standing with her legs spread shoulder width apart, Ami waited for him to open the register.

She nodded her head toward the counter. "All of it. Even what's under the drawer and in the safe. Put it in a bag. I need this money for a new dress. This one's covered in cum."

The man's hands full of bills, he reached under the register for a bag. As his hand came above the bottom of the counter, Ami caught a glimpse of something metallic and shiny.

Immediately, and without a moment's thought, she pulled the trigger.

The explosion was deafening inside the small store.

The right side of the man's head exploded, splattering the glass behind the register with brain matter and blood. As he fell backward, he dropped the shotgun on the floor beside where he had been standing.

"Still here," Ami shouted.

"That's my girl," Ryan said.

Ryan walked toward the register, alternating glances between the door and where Ami stood.

He peered over the counter and down at the man. Half of his head was gone, leaving a disproportionate skull with only one eye. His eyes widened and his mouth twisted into a smirk. "Son-of-a-bitch, what a fucking mess."

A six-foot wide splatter of blood and brain matter covered the glass wall behind the counter.

"Well, you should have seen the size of his head, it's huge." She leaned over the counter and looked down at the now dead man's half missing head. "Well, it *was* huge."

Ami tossed her head toward the rear of the store. "Grab a couple

Red Bull's and a sack of Chicharones, and I'll get the money."

She jumped onto the countertop.

"*Chee cha what's?*" Ryan asked over his shoulder as he walked toward the beverage cooler.

"Chicharones," Ami shouted as she hopped down off of the counter.

She landed directly into the puddle of blood, slipping and falling twice.

"Awe fuck," she shouted.

Ami braced herself from completely falling again by thrusting her hands in front of her into the puddle of blood. Crouched on the floor in the puddle of blood and brain matter, she attempted to pick up the money from the floor. As she did, her hair continuously fell into her eyes. Frustrated, she brushed her hair behind her ear with her hand. Unbeknownst to her, her bloody hand slid along the side of her face, leaving a large bloody streak.

With her hand that held the pistol, she wiped her sweat-soaked brow, leaving another bloody streak across her forehead.

"What happened?" Ryan shouted.

"Guts. I stepped in guts," she said. "No biggie."

With bloody hands, she picked up each and every bill.

"And they're pork fat," Ami shouted. "Fried forkfats."

Standing at the cooler, Ryan turned to face Ami and made eye contact. As he stood with his hands full of Red Bull, he raised his eyebrows in wonder.

She chuckled. "Pigskins. Fucking pork rinds. Whatever the fuck you wanna call 'em. They're low fat, low sodium, and high in protein."

"That's one of the things I love about you, baby. Through all of this, you're health conscious," Ryan shouted.

"That, and I'll kill a motherfucker who gets in the way of my shopping habit," Ami said with a laugh.

Ryan nodded. "That too."

"Headlights," Ryan shouted.

"For fuck's sake," Ami screamed as she stepped over the counter, one hand full of blood-covered money, the other bloody hand holding her pistol.

She turned to face Ryan. Her face, hands and arms were covered in blood. Ryan shook his head at the sight of her. As a vehicle pulled up alongside the gas pumps, his eyes shifted quickly to the parking lot.

The driver got out and began to attempt to pump fuel.

Ryan turned to face Ami. "You look like you've…"

He paused and shook his head as he studied the amount of blood that covered Ami.

"Been to hell and back?" Ami asked.

"Precisely," Ryan responded.

She grinned. "Only for you, Baby."

Her eyes, too, shifted toward the car at the gas pumps.

The driver, frustrated because the now dead attendant had not set the pump to be operational, began to walk toward the store entrance. As he approached, he stared down at his feet, shaking his head in frustration.

"Looks like he's coming in," Ryan whispered.

Ami began to walk toward the door, her gun held steady at arm's length. As she got within a few feet of the door, the approaching man looked up and noticed Ami, the gun, blood, and money.

His eyes widened.

He turned and began to run toward the car.

"Grab my fucking pigskins," Ami screamed over her shoulder.

Without hesitation, Ami opened the door, extended her arm, and took aim.

"*Run motherfucker*," Ami whispered as she looked down the barrel of the pistol.

She chuckled as he reached for the door handle of the car.

"Fuck it, you're gonna die anyway," she said softly.

And she pulled the trigger.

www.ingramcontent.com/pod-product-compliance
Lightning Source LLC
Chambersburg PA
CBHW050729180626
46814CB00002B/671